THE FOUR OLDER CHILDREN WENT STRAIGHT DOWN TO THE FIRST COVE AND MADE THEIR WAY BY THE
ROCKS TO THEIR DESTINATION (Chap. 3)

BEGINNING
AT BANSTONE

PRISCILLA NAISH

LONDON
PICKERING & INGLIS LTD.
1962

PICKERING & INGLIS LTD.

29 LUDGATE HILL, LONDON, E.C.4
229 BOTHWELL STREET, GLASGOW, C.2
Home Evangel Books Ltd., 25 Hobson Avenue, Toronto, 16

Made and Printed in Great Britain

CONTENTS

CHAPTER I

INTRODUCING THE CHALLENGERS

RICHARD leaned across from where he was lying in his sleeping bag, to the other side of the tent towards Paul and shook him hard by the shoulder.

"Wake up, lazybones!" he said. "Tony and I have been awake for ages. It's Sunday, don't forget, and Daddy promised to take us for an early morning bathe. It must be nearly time. Besides, today's the day the mission starts."

Paul stretched himself luxuriously, turned over slowly in his sleeping bag towards the door of the tent and lifted the flap to look out. What he saw did not encourage him. It was still very early, in spite of what Richard had said, and there was a thick mist which would have discouraged any but the keenest bather.

"It can't be time yet," he grumbled. "And anyway, it's all very well for you to talk about the mission, but how do I know I shall like it? It all sounds a bit cissy to me."

"Oo, it isn't!" exclaimed Tony. He was only seven but was always ready to take up the cudgels on behalf of anything or anyone he liked.

"We have all sorts of super things," he went on. "Treasure-hunts, sausage sizzles, and—and lots of other things." Words failed him as he tried to remember all the variety of entertainment they had enjoyed when they had come to Banstone the previous year.

"Steady on, Tony," said Richard, "or Paul will think we're having all those today." He turned to Paul and went on to explain, "Of course, we don't have any of those things on Sunday, but there's the service on the beach this afternoon for children and parents and we all go, and it's ever so interesting, much more even than church at home."

"I should jolly well hope it would be more interesting than church. I can't stick church myself. Can't think why anybody goes who hasn't got to!"

Tony looked at Paul in astonishment. "Well, you ought to come with us. There's special children's church which Richard and me and Anne and Elizabeth go to while Daddy and Mummy go into the grown-up service."

Richard chimed in. "Yes, and even the grown-up service is quite interesting, too, in our church. I sometimes go in with Mummy and Daddy now that I'm eleven."

While they went on talking about church and the mission, Richard and Tony explaining to Paul all the things that went on at both, the mist began to clear outside and gradually the sun became visible through the tent walls and heralded another beautiful day.

Richard and Tony Challenger and Richard's school friend, Paul Taylor, aged eleven, were camping with Mr. and Mrs. Challenger and the other two members of the family, Anne aged nine and Elizabeth aged four, at the small seaside village of Banstone. The three boys were occupying a small ridge tent, while Mr. and Mrs. Challenger and the girls slept in the large bell tent, which was also used as a living-tent on the occasions when it was too wet or cold to be out of doors. It had been a wonderful summer, though, and the big tent had rarely had to be used in the day-time. The weather indeed had been almost too hot and Mrs. Challenger often had to warn the children not to stay too long in their costumes after swimming. Already some of them had had a few very uncomfortable nights with backs and necks sore from too much sun.

Paul Taylor had been in the same class as Richard at the junior school at home and they were next term starting together at the local grammar school. Paul's parents were tea-planters in Ceylon and, as he had no hope of a holiday by the sea and only the company of the elderly aunt with whom he lived, for the six weeks of the summer holidays, Mr. and Mrs. Challenger had taken pity on him and asked permission for him to join them in their three weeks' camp by the sea.

Paul had never known a Christian family until he met the Challengers. He went to church, but unfortunately it was not a church which made any provision for young people. They were expected to join in the adult services, if they went at all, and no attempt was made to explain things to them, so consequently they soon lost interest. The adults who attended the church were good-living people who always agreed with everything that was said in the sermon on Sundays, but never let it make any difference to the lives they lived during the week.

Richard, who had grown up in a home where Christianity belonged to every day of the week, when he first came to know Paul was secretly quite shocked at the things he used to say about Church and the Bible from time to time. He had trusted the Lord Jesus Christ for himself the previous year at the Banstone mission, and was most anxious that Paul should do the same this year.

As the church clock was striking seven, Mr. Challenger banged on the outside of the boys' tent.

"Are you boys awake? It's time you were if you want that bathe! Or are you shirking it?"

"Daddy! We've been awake ages," came Tony's protest from inside.

"All right then! Get your trunks and gym shoes on quickly and come to our tent. But be quiet about it. Elizabeth is still asleep and we don't want to wake her yet, if possible."

But it was no good. By the time the boys reached the bell tent Elizabeth, obviously only just awake, was climbing sleepily out of her sleeping bag and saying, "Can't I come too, Daddy? Mummy, can't I go?"

She liked to feel that she was big enough to go with the older children but secretly she was a little afraid of the bigger waves which broke on the main beach, and Mrs. Challenger, realising this, said quickly, "But Elizabeth, I thought you were going to help me to get the breakfast while the others bathe. I need someone to work Dobbin for me."

Dobbin was a much-loved egg-timer, which had a horse's head on it, hence its name, and it was Elizabeth's great joy to set the glass in position and watch the sand sift through slowly and then to tell Mummy when the eggs were done. Mrs. Challenger further added to her persuasion by saying, "Besides, I want to bathe myself later today near the causeway. It's so nice and smooth there and much warmer. And who will come with me if you don't?"

Elizabeth heaved a sigh of relief and said, "Oo yes! I'll bathe with you later and then I can help with breakfast now."

When the bathers had gone, Mrs. Challenger, helped by Elizabeth, laid out groundsheets on the grass outside the big tent, rolled the sleeping bags into bundles for the family to sit on at breakfast time, and then proceeded to prepare the breakfast. Coffee and boiled eggs was always the rule for Sunday breakfast at home and this could not be changed just because they were in camp. The coffee for the children was nearly all milk, but was still a special treat; on weekdays they had plain milk while Mr. and Mrs. Challenger had tea.

Elizabeth watched her mother while she lit the two Primus stoves. She always liked waiting for the moment when Mummy pumped them and they suddenly flared into action and were ready to be used. Then she half-filled the egg pan with water from the canvas bucket while Mummy put milk, and coffee which had been standing in the big jug since the night before, into a saucepan.

"Lay the tablecloth on the groundsheet, Elizabeth, and get out the plates, mugs and egg-cups while we're waiting for the egg water to boil."

When these jobs were done, Elizabeth and her mother sat down to wait for the time when Dobbin could be put into action, and to watch the path along which the rest of the family would soon come back from their morning bathe.

CHAPTER II

MR. CHALLENGER SURPRISED

A S the bathers walked down the path to the beach, Paul and Tony took Mr. Challenger on ahead, while Richard drew Anne behind to unfold to her a plan the boys had made when they had been getting ready for the bathe.

"We've got an idea for ducking Daddy—you know he's always got away so far. Well, you remember Paul and I were practising duck-diving and swimming under water yesterday? You and Tony have got to make Daddy take you both a little way out, and while his back's turned we're going to dive and catch his legs and pull him down, and you Tony must pull his arms. You'll know when to do it, because Daddy's legs will give way. Do be sure to do the job properly. We must get him down this time!"

There was, of course, the usual unwillingness about actually getting into the water; Anne was particularly slow and loud in her protestations that the water was much too cold. But eventually they were all in and Tony said, with an excitement he could hardly conceal, "Daddy, do take Anne and me out a bit further. You hardly ever do, and you know you won't let us go by ourselves."

"All right son," said his father unsuspectingly. "But you must hold my hand, remember."

Nothing could have suited them better, and the three of them moved further into the water, Anne and Tony trying hard not to look behind to see if Richard and Paul were following. They had not long to wait. Quite suddenly Mr. Challenger gave a yell, jumped a little in the water and then began to plunge wildly, trying hard to free himself from four pairs of hands that were ruthlessly pulling him down. After very little struggle he gave up trying to escape and went under as gracefully as he could, upon which the children released him and stood round laughing and cheering.

"At last we've beaten you!" shouted Tony.

"Yes, all right. You win! I know when I'm done!" said his father. "All the same, you won't do that trick on each other, will you? Or there might be trouble. Anyone who is not a very strong swimmer might just lose their head if they were held under like that. You'll be careful, won't you?"

The older ones agreed immediately but Tony was jumping up and down in the water with such glee that he was not listening. His father caught hold of him and held him still for a moment.

"Did you hear, Tony? You mustn't do that to other people, mind! We don't want any accidents."

"All right, Daddy," said Tony, cheerfully. "I don't mind now we've got you down!"

"You little wretch!" said Mr. Challenger, then he added, "Now then, children, only a few minutes more or Mummy will be waiting with the breakfast and our eggs will be cold."

So, after another five minutes they waded out to the shore, rubbed themselves as dry as possible with towels, put on their gym shoes and set off at a brisk pace up the path towards the camp site.

Paul hung back a little. The other children were all laughing and joking with their father and he noticed again, as he had several times since he had come to Banstone with the Challengers, that Mr. Challenger seemed to treat the children almost as equals, and that they did not seem to stand in the slightest awe of him. He had been almost afraid to agree when the plans were made to duck Mr. Challenger earlier that morning. He had quite expected him to be angry, at least for a few moments, or, worse still, that it might get them all into serious trouble and spoil the whole day. He knew better than to try any practical jokes with his aunt, who believed that children should be seen and not heard, and it was so long since he had seen his parents that he had forgotten all about the fun of normal family life. He thought all grown-ups were rather like his aunt, never taking much notice of him except to punish him when he was naughty, and to see that he had all he needed in the way of food, clothing and other necessities. He had letters from his parents of course, but they had not seen him for six years and did not seem to know how to write to a boy of eleven. Paul, in his turn, never knew what to write about to fill his weekly air letter form; he wrote as large as he could, but even with that the last side was always a great effort. He did not realise that they would be interested in the day-to-day happenings at school.

The longer Paul stayed with the Challengers, the more at home and one of the family he felt, and as he thought about it that morning he made a sudden resolve not to do anything which would displease the parents or be a bad example to the other children. Then he ran up the path after the others, catching up on them just as they reached the camp site, where Elizabeth and Mrs. Challenger had breakfast nearly ready.

CHAPTER III

THE START OF THE MISSION

THE service which the boys had been talking about before they got up was held in one of the small rocky coves, of which there were several in Banstone. A path ran along the head of the coves and there were steps down to each one. When the tide was out it was possible to walk along the beach from cove to cove, but at high tide they were cut off from each other. The rocks between could be climbed, and the children usually went that way, but older and less athletic people would climb up the steps, walk along the path and climb down again if they wanted to move to another cove when the tide was in. This is what happened on Sunday afternoon. The Challenger family and Paul walked down to the path, from the field where the camp was. Then the four older children went straight down to the first cove and made their way by the rocks to their destination. Mr. and Mrs. Challenger and Elizabeth, who was still too small for rock-climbing, went along the top and down the steps to Smugglers' Cove.

No-one knew where this particular cove got its name. The local inhabitants, when asked, could only say that it had always been called that, within living memory. The children were always hoping to find some cave or secret hoard which would prove that there had actually been smugglers there in earlier days, but so far they had not been successful. However, nothing daunted, they continued their efforts and Smugglers' Cove was always a favourite spot.

Mr. and Mrs. Challenger and Elizabeth reached the cove first and, although it was more than fifteen minutes before the service was due to start, a small crowd of children and adults had already gathered. The Challengers knew several of them from the previous year when they had spent their holidays also in Banstone, particularly some of the members of the team of workers who were running the mission which was just starting. They were greeted almost immediately by Mr. and Mrs. Johnson, the leader and his wife, who had a family of four children of similar ages to the Challenger family. Elizabeth, who was too young to remember them from the year before, was rather shy at first, but soon overcame her shyness and was chattering happily to Pauline, the youngest, aged five. Very shortly the rest of the Challengers and Paul climbed down from the rocks which bounded the cove on the right, and came running across the sands.

"Hullo, you lot," called Mr. Johnson. "Nice to be back at Banstone again, isn't it? Your father tells me you have been here a week already. Ah well, it's nice to be some people. How are you all?"

"Very well, thank you, Mr. Johnson," said Richard, the spokesman of the party. "This is my friend, Paul Taylor, who's camping with us."

"How do you do, Paul? I'm glad to see you at Banstone and to welcome you to the mission," said Mr. Johnson, while the other children turned to Mrs. Johnson.

"Where are Judith and the others, Mrs. Johnson?" asked Anne. "Have they come down yet?"

"Yes, there they are, Anne," said Mrs. Johnson, pointing. "And Elizabeth has made friends with Pauline already." She turned to Richard and Tony. "The boys have been counting the days to see you two. I think they have some new idea about the smugglers!"

"Hurrah! Come on, Paul. Come and meet Colin and Peter."

The three boys, followed by Anne, moved to where Mrs.

Johnson had pointed, and soon Paul found himself being introduced to the three Johnson children, Colin, aged twelve, Judith, aged nine, and Peter, aged seven.

"Peter and I are nearly twins," said Tony. "Only he is a week older than I am," he added regretfully, for this was a sore point with him. He had wished over and over again that it was the other way about. Peter could always be relied upon to use his age as a final weapon if he was losing in one of the many arguments he and Tony had together. The parents of the two boys were agreed that it was probably fortunate that they did not meet very often, as they seemed to cross swords so easily.

Paul liked the look of Colin immediately, but was not much interested in Judith because she was a girl, or in Peter, because he was so young; he considered them both beneath his notice. There was no time just then to get to know Colin any further as the service was obviously just about to start and Paul sat down with the others, wondering just what to expect.

He was pleasantly surprised. The service was far from being childish, or boring, as he had feared it might be, and when it finished he was amazed to find the time had gone so quickly. The children sat in a group together on the sand. Some of the grown-ups sat with them, while others had procured deck chairs and enjoyed more comfort. They sang hymns from printed sheets and also what Mr. Johnson called 'choruses', which seemed to Paul like short hymns, only rather easier to understand. They had no copies of the words for these and Paul felt rather embarrassed because he thought eveyone would see that he did not know them. But he need not have worried. There were evidently others who did not know them either and Mr. Johnson repeated the words of each one before they sang it. This set Paul's mind at rest and he knew that he would soon learn them.

There were two prayers during the service, one after the first hymn and one at the end. Again Paul was surprised and relieved. He realised that they were not like church prayers but like those Mr. Challenger always prayed after they had read the Bible at breakfast time in camp. While Paul had at first felt that this daily Bible reading and prayer was very odd and a complete waste of time, he now quite enjoyed it and even looked forward to it. Mr. Challenger made the Bible so simple when he explained it, and when he prayed— well, Paul had never heard anything like it! He talked to God as if He were quite close, instead of a long way off, and about the most ordinary things, thanking Him for when they had had a good time, perhaps at a picnic or a game of beach-cricket and asking Him for help for even quite small things.

After various announcements had been made about the next day's activities, Mr. Johnson began to talk to them and Paul supposed that this was the same as the sermon in church. He decided that he would not bother to listen—he never liked sermon time at home. He gazed around him, at the sand, the rocks, the sea, and the people, and began to think again about the smugglers. He wondered about the new idea the Johnsons had, and as he did so his eyes roamed round the cove again, looking for hiding places or blocked entrances to caves. He decided, for perhaps the fiftieth time since he had come to Banstone, that there was nothing new to see and came out of his daydream to hear Mr. Johnson saying, "It's something that no-one else can do for you; you have to decide for yourself whether you will accept what the Lord Jesus Christ did for you. And you know, if you don't accept and say 'Thank you', it's just the same as saying 'I don't want it'."

Almost immediately after Mr. Johnson finished speaking, one of the other workers gave out a hymn and after it had been sung the service finished with a prayer.

Paul was again introduced to various friends whom the Challengers had met at Banstone the previous year. There were several of the mission workers: a Mr. Henderson, who was a Cambridge cricketer and a great favourite with all the children; Mr. Collier, who, Paul heard afterwards, told wonderful stories; Miss Wentworth, who was cooking for the workers; and some others whose names Paul could not take in at the time—as well as a number of children.

After a few minutes Mr. Challenger came up and said, "Elizabeth and Mummy are going to have their bathe by the causeway, and as they got breakfast for us this morning while we bathed we are going to get tea for them. That's what I call division of labour."

"Not a very good division," said Mrs. Challenger, coming up behind him at that moment. "Five of you to get tea, and only two of us this morning to get breakfast which is a much bigger meal. Mind you do the job properly!"

They all laughed and the two parties separated, Mr. Challenger and the older children going towards the camp site, and Mrs. Challenger and Elizabeth making for the causeway, which was round the corner in the estuary, where there were very few waves and the sea was the right depth and temperature for Elizabeth to enjoy.

As they walked along, Mr. Challenger and the children chatted together about all the old and new friends they had seen at the service. Then Tony said,

"I say, all of you, did you notice that boy and girl sitting up on the rocks at the side listening to the service? Weren't they the ones we saw hanging about on Friday when we were rock-climbing?"

"Yes, I saw them too, Tony," answered his father. "I think they are the same, though we didn't get very close to them on Friday so it's a bit hard to tell."

"I wonder who they are," mused Richard. "They look a

2

bit scruffy, if you ask me. Wonder what they were doing at the service."

"They've as much right to be at the service as we have, Richard," replied Mr. Challenger. "And if they are a bit unkempt, it may not be their fault. They look as if they are twins, both having very fair hair and blue eyes, although the boy seems a bit bigger. They look almost foreign, too, don't they?"

At this point they reached camp and all set to work to get tea ready. When Mrs. Challenger returned with Elizabeth it was all ready waiting.

Mr. Challenger said to his wife, "I thought we started a new loaf and packet of butter at breakfast this morning."

"So we did," replied Mrs. Challenger. "I put them in the usual place in the store tent."

"Well, they're not there now."

"Are you sure?" asked Mrs. Challenger, going to look. When she returned from the store tent she said, "You're quite right. They've disappeared. I wonder whoever could have taken them!"

As they gathered round for tea, they all, even Elizabeth, discussed with great seriousness who the thief could be.

CHAPTER IV

MONDAY MORNING

THE next morning dawned fine and clear and the children were up in good time to do all the camp chores before going to the beach service at ten o'clock. First the tents had to be tidied, the sides tied up neatly, the bedding taken out to air during breakfast and later folded up. Then the canvas buckets had to be filled with water from the tap on the cliff path and the milk fetched from the farm. After breakfast the washing-up had to be done and the vegetables prepared for dinner. Each of the children knew what was required and they worked with a will, as they were all anxious to be at Smuggler's Cove early to help to build and decorate the sand pulpit for the service.

At ten o'clock they set out, the boys all carrying their spades and going on ahead, and Anne and Elizabeth following more slowly, gathering flowers as they went. Mr. and Mrs. Challenger stayed behind; they were going to the village to do the shopping and would come down to the cove later.

When the boys reached the site only a very few children had arrived but Mr. Johnson and a worker they did not know had already started digging a pulpit. Mr. Johnson looked up as they came down the steps—they had gone by the path to save time—and said, "Good for you, you three. I'm glad you've got spades. We've only the two we brought down, and we could do with some extra help."

"Anne and Elizabeth are gathering flowers to decorate the pulpit, Mr. Johnson," said Tony. "Where are Mr. Henderson and Mr. Collier?"

"They are giving out programmes along towards Penton in the hope of meeting people coming here for the day. Meanwhile, this is Mr. Stanton who has never been to a mission before. You'll be able to show him a thing or two, won't you? Mr. Stanton, this is Richard and Tony Challenger and their friend Paul—I'm afraid I can't remember your other name, Paul, though I know Richard told me yesterday."

"Taylor," said Paul, rather shyly, and then to cover his embarrassment, "Can we help to dig? Or what would you like us to do?"

"Yes, of course," replied Mr. Johnson. "Would you three go round the other side and dig along the line I've marked, throwing the sand towards us. Mind you're not too energetic with it, though. We don't want to have to put it all back into the middle, nor do we want it in our eyes!"

The three boys worked energetically for a short time but Tony soon tired and gave up his spade to a boy standing nearby who wanted a turn. It was not very long before a fair-sized mound was raised and then they all began to pat it flat with the backs of their spades. Two steps were cut out at the back and Richard and Paul went to find large stones to put on them to make them firm. Just as the pulpit building was nearly finished, Mrs. Johnson and another worker, Miss Conway, came down the steps with a small crowd of children, most of them carrying flowers, and among them were Anne and Elizabeth.

"Do you know what the text is?" Anne was asking.

"No, Anne, we'll have to ask Mr. Johnson. He's sure to know," replied Mrs. Johnson.

Anne walked across to Mr. Johnson, still holding Elizabeth by the hand. She had promised Mummy to look after her.

"Mr. Johnson, Mrs. Johnson wants to know what the text is, please."

At that moment Mrs. Johnson came up behind and Mr. Johnson said to them both, "Just a minute, let me get the sand off my hands. I'll have to look it up in my diary. Mr. Collier put it in there for me just before I came down."

"Oo, is Mr. Collier going to talk to us this morning?" asked Anne. "He always tells such wizard stories."

"Yes, it's Mr. Collier this morning, and his text to put on the pulpit is 'He leadeth me'," said Mr. Johnson, after opening his diary. "Do you know where that comes from, Anne? You'd probably remember it better if I told you the whole verse. 'He maketh me to lie down in green pastures; he leadeth me beside the still waters'."

"Yes, I know that," said Anne. "It's Psalm 23. I recited it in Sunday School a few weeks ago. We have what's called a roll of honour and when we've done twelve things, like reciting something from the Bible, singing a hymn, or bringing a new scholar, the roll of honour is framed and we can hang it up. I've got one above my bed and I'm just starting on my second."

"That's a good idea," said Mrs. Johnson. "Have you started one yet, Elizabeth?"

"Yes," replied Elizabeth, almost in a whisper. She was very quiet when talking to grown-ups, though by now she could make plenty of noise with Pauline. As often happened, Anne spoke for her.

"She's only in the primary, so they are allowed to sing choruses for their roll of honour and she has quite a lot on hers already."

"Well, keep it up, both of you," said Mrs. Johnson. "And now we really must get on with the decorating."

Mrs. Johnson marked out the words of the text with the corner of the spade and then the girls started filling in the letters with flower heads of various kinds. There had been an abundance of knapweed along the side of the path by which they had come and this made the letters stand out nicely, and soon, even from the path above, it was possible to read the words. Someone had brought a bag of shells and these were used to fill in the capital letter and to make a border.

"Whoever managed to find those shells?" asked Mrs. Johnson. "There are none in Banstone, I'm sure, because Judith and I spent a long time looking one afternoon last year."

"They come from Warstead, across the estuary, Mrs. Johnson," said a girl named Susan, who had long fair hair. "Mummy and Daddy took me there last Tuesday—we've been here a week already—and there were so many shells, I just had to collect some. I remembered how we wanted them once or twice last year."

"What a good idea, Susan," said Mrs. Johnson. "We must take them out after the service and keep them for another time, if you will let us."

"Yes, of course," agreed Susan. "That's what I thought."

By this time the pulpit was ready. Bunches of the flowers left over were arranged along the top and the effect was very pretty. Quite a large crowd of children had gathered, but not so many adults as on the previous day. Some of the children had made themselves pews out of sand, while others contented themselves with sitting directly on the sand and stretching their legs out in front and digging their heels into the sand for added comfort. A boy was giving out hymn-books and a girl chorus-books, and when everyone was settled the service began.

Mr. Henderson was doing most of the talking this time, giving out the hymns, praying, leading the choruses, and the service was rather similar to the Sunday one. It was still interesting, though, and Paul decided he would listen to the talk when it came. The others were right, Mr. Collier did know how to tell stories. He talked about a mountain which could only be climbed with the help of a guide, and then told them of various mountaineers who relied on other people or things to take them to the top, and of course failed to get there. One depended on his friends but they were no better able than he was to reach the summit; another trusted in his map, but he was not able to read it very well and so lost his way; yet another decided that the local people would be able to tell him the way, but none of them had been up themselves; and another had undergone intensive training and thought that his physical fitness and endurance alone would take him there. But it was only those who followed the guide, obeyed his instructions and had complete confidence in him, who ever arrived at the top.

Mr. Collier told this story in such an exciting way that all the children sat enthralled, almost open-mouthed, as they listened. Then he began to show that the story had a meaning, that the way of life is like that journey up the mountain, and can never be accomplished successfully without the only guide, the Lord Jesus Christ. He ended the talk by quoting in full Psalm 23 from which the text on the pulpit had come. Paul rather resented this ending to such an interesting talk. Surely he could manage his life by himself. He got on very well as it was and he had no parents near at hand to help him like most children, and he did not consider that his aunt was of very much use. Paul was of a very independent nature and liked to think he could live his own life, without help from anyone. He decided that, much as he liked Mr. Collier's talk to begin with, the ending had spoilt it all.

He managed to forget about it during the rest of the day as there was so much else to do. After the beach service there was bathing organised by the mission workers and the older children stayed for it. When it was announced, they were rather dismayed because they had not brought their bathing costumes and towels and they thought that by the time they had been back to camp for them, the swim would be almost over. However, at this moment, Mr. and Mrs. Challenger appeared with bathing togs for them all, much to their delight. Mr. Challenger had remembered that the previous year there had often been organised bathing after the morning service, and after he and Mrs. Challenger had done the shopping they had gone back to camp to leave what they had bought, and gathered up all the towels and bathing costumes from the line where they always hung in fine weather.

CHAPTER V

AFTERNOON GAMES

IN the afternoon the children attending the mission gathered on the beach, each age group in a different cove, and played games together, under the charge of the workers. Paul and Richard were intermediates and played a game which was new to Paul, called 'Crocker', using a football, cricket stumps and a baseball bat. Colin Johnson, who was also in their age group, was one of the best players there and Paul and Richard were glad to be in his team. He seemed to score most of the runs for their side and they easily won the game. While others of the team were batting, Paul and Richard sat with Colin and they all chattered together about everything under the sun. By the end of the afternoon Paul had a great admiration for Colin and was looking forward to seeing a great deal of him during the next two weeks.

They also had in their team the two children they had talked about on the way home from the Sunday service. Paul had not noticed them at the morning service and had forgotten about them. But they joined in the game with great enthusiasm, although they only talked between themselves and not to the other children. Paul discovered that their names were Hans and Gerda and once, at an exciting moment in the game, Mr. Henderson shouted out, "Catch it, twin!"

"So Mr. Challenger was right," thought Paul. "They are twins, and from the sound of their names they might well be foreign too."

Anne and Tony joined the juniors, although Tony was still only tiny-tot age, and played rounders, and then 'halo' with a rubber ring and a net. Elizabeth overcame her shyness and went with Pauline to play with the tiny-tots. They played a variety of games of the kind that small children love, including 'Oranges and Lemons', 'Wolf, wolf, come over here', and others like them.

The games' session was an opportunity for the children to get to know each other in their own age group and it worked well. They arrived back in camp at teatime, full of the new friends they had made and the games they had played.

Mr. Challenger was stretched out in a deck-chair, while Mrs. Challenger was getting the tea ready.

"Daddy!" cried Anne, "have you been like that all afternoon?"

Mr. Challenger snorted. "Go and look over in the corner at the rubbish pit and the grease pit and then you'll see what I've been doing all afternoon. All that digging on a hot afternoon while you've been playing. I shall expect to be waited on at tea to make up for it, in fact I don't think I shall recover in time to do my washing-up."

Anne went across to the corner of the field and found that the old grease pit and rubbish pit had been filled in and the turf replaced neatly. A little to one side were two new empty pits ready for rubbish and greasy water. Anne went back to her father and patted him on the back, saying teasingly, "All right, Daddy, you have been working hard, and I'm quite sure you won't want any tea after that—you'll need to rest instead, won't you?"

"Baggage!" said her father and he pulled her down on top of him and held her there, struggling, until Mrs. Challenger called that tea was ready.

At teatime Mrs. Challenger told them that two of the spare blankets which she had put out to air on the line before they went to the service had gone.

"You don't remember noticing whether they were there at dinner time, do you children?" she asked.

"No, I'm sure they weren't there," said Anne immediately. "Because Tony and I were playing tag round the posts just before dinner."

"Then they must have gone while we were all at the service in the morning, because I definitely put them there when Daddy and I collected the bathing things."

"What shall we do without them, Mummy?" asked Elizabeth.

"Well, as long as the weather stays like this, we don't need them. But if it gets colder I don't know what we shall do. And anyway, we can't afford to lose two blankets."

"Oughtn't we to go to the police, Daddy?" asked Richard.

"I don't think we'll do that just yet," said Mr. Challenger thoughtfully. "I think we'll wait to see if there are any further developments."

When tea was over it was time for Elizabeth to go to bed. Six o'clock was her bedtime, seven o'clock Tony's and Anne's, and Richard and Paul came last at eight o'clock.

Just as Paul was dropping off to sleep he heard Richard exclaim, "Bother!"

"What's up?" murmured Paul sleepily.

"I forgot to ask Colin what their idea was about Smugglers' Cove. We must find out from them tomorrow."

CHAPTER VI

ELIZABETH'S TREASURE

ON Tuesday afternoon the tiny tots had a treasure hunt. Mr. Collier told them first about a wicked goblin who had raided a teddybear's storehouse and carried away a large treasure trove of chocolate and hidden it in what he thought was a safe place. In case he could not find the place when he wanted it, the goblin had laid a trail of dried peas to it and somehow Mr. Collier had found this out and wanted the children to follow the trail with him to see if they could find the treasure. They set off, looking as they went along for the little piles of dried peas the goblin had left. Mr. Collier warned them that they must not let the passers-by know what they were doing in case any of them were friends of the goblin and told him. So they pretended that they were looking for flowers and some of them even picked small bunches, to hide what they were really doing. The trail led them by a very roundabout route to the sand pits above Smugglers' Cove and there it stopped.

The children looked all round to make sure that it continued no further and then Mr. Collier said, "Well, it looks as if the treasure must be somewhere here. How many of you have brought spades? I thought we might have to dig, that's why I told you to bring them."

Half a dozen of the tots set to work under Mr. Collier's direction, while the others made what they thought were helpful suggestions. Suddenly Elizabeth, who was standing by Pauline, nudged her and whispered, because she did not like to speak out when everyone was so quite, "Look, Pauline, what's that dark thing up there?"

Pauline was not shy and at once said to Mr. Collier in great excitement, "Mr. Collier, Elizabeth's just seen something. Is it the treasure?" And they both pointed to the bank where the end of a block of wrapped chocolate had been uncovered when the sand, disturbed by the digging, had slipped down into the pit.

"Up you go, Elizabeth, and see what it is," said Mr. Collier. "It looks as if you'll have the first find."

Elizabeth scrambled up the rather steep sand bank, dislodging some more sand as she went, and, when she reached the point where she thought the treasure was, she found that two objects had been uncovered. She pulled these out and found that they were two-ounce blocks of chocolate. When she came down to the bottom again the other children were all very excited and a little envious.

"Is that all the treasure?" they asked Mr. Collier, rather sorrowfully.

"Oh no! There must be plenty more. Do you think the goblin would take all that trouble for just two bars? Come on, you diggers, get moving. We must find it before he comes to look for it himself."

They dug on and eventually uncovered a little store of chocolate bars by the end of the afternoon. As there were not enough for them to have one each, the bars were broken up and shared out. While they were munching happily, Mr. Collier said, "You'd better not tell your mothers you've had this now or they'll think it will spoil your tea. Isn't it funny that anyone should think a few pieces of chocolate could spoil your tea? I'm sure it would take more than that to spoil mine!"

When they separated to go home, Mr. Collier warned, "I expect when the goblin finds out that his treasure has gone he'll want his revenge, so we'll have to be careful. He won't think it is you children, but the workers will have to watch their step."

CHAPTER VII

PREPARATION FOR ADVENTURE

THAT night when the older boys were getting ready for bed Richard said to Tony,

"We asked Colin what their idea was about the smugglers this afternoon. We were on the same side in cricket and while we were waiting to bat he told us. You know the steps down to the Cove? Well, as they were going down to the beach when they first arrived on Saturday they noticed where the steps bend that there is a gap between the steps and the cliff, and then they looked lower down and found another like it and they're wondering if those steps hide some sort of passage. There's only sand in some places and they thought that if we could dig there we'd find the opening."

"I say, how wizard!" exclaimed Tony. "When are you going to dig? You'll have to find a time when there's no one around."

"Well, as a matter of fact, we've arranged to meet Colin and Peter there after dark tonight," said Richard.

"Richard! And you've kept quiet about it ever since this afternoon? Why didn't you tell me? I'm coming too!"

"You'd have blabbed it all out at teatime if we'd told you, and you've got to promise not to say anything if we let you come tonight."

"I know how to keep a secret. Of course I wouldn't have blabbed." said Tony indignantly.

"Huh!" retorted Richard. "What about that airgun? Anyway, are you going to promise?"

"Yes, course I'll promise. And it's not fair to bring that up. I was years younger then."

"Only one year, and you don't seem much wiser now," retorted Richard. He was still rather bitter about the incident. Their father had forbidden them to have guns of any kind on the grounds of safety, and he had been lent one by a boy from school to try out. He had brought it home secretly for just one night and Tony had let the cat out of the bag so that his father found out and took it away from him. He had not even had one shot with it, and he had been punished by his father, too.

"All right, I've promised, haven't I? What time are we going?" asked Tony.

"We're meeting Colin and Peter at half-past ten at the steps. It will be dark then and no one will be about, and I said Daddy and Mummy went to bed at ten o'clock, so it ought to be quite easy."

"What about Colin and Peter? However will they get out of the Mission House, with so many people about?"

"Oh, didn't you know?" asked Richard. "The house is so full this year that they are sleeping in a tent in the garden, so it's even better for them."

At this point Paul asked, rather hesitantly, "Richard, are you sure it's all right to go out of camp without permission?"

Richard laughed. "Daddy and Mummy won't know, silly, and it can't do any harm. We won't be out too long, but I'm just wondering if we ought to take Tony."

"You're not going to leave me out now," protested Tony. "I should blab if you did that! Come on, Richard, tell me how you're going to wake up, and how you'll know the time. We've none of us got watches."

"Well," said Richard, relenting. "Paul and I thought we'd take it in turns—it's only just over two hours and if we do an hour each, it should be all right. We'll know the time because at night and in the early morning you can hear the church clock striking. You hardly ever hear it in the day because of the noise from people on the beach and the cliff path. But you've heard it in the morning sometimes, haven't you? And Paul and I have often heard if after we were in bed. One of us will stay awake till just after nine, and then wake the other, who will stay awake till they see the light go out in the big tent. Then we'll wait about another ten minutes, and crawl out under the flaps at the back of our tent away from Daddy and Mummy."

"Are you getting undressed?" asked Tony. "Ought I to get my clothes on again now and go to bed in them?"

"We're only taking off our shorts and sweaters and leaving all the rest on. You can do what you like." Richard was secretly hoping that Tony would not wake up and they could go without him, and, truth to tell, so was Paul. He felt uncertain enough about doing anything which would displease Mr. and Mrs. Challenger, and he did not think Tony should have been brought into it at all. The Challengers were being very decent to him, having him to camp with them for all this time—he had never enjoyed a holiday so much in all the years his parents had been away—and he had an uneasy conscience about carrying out this plan that Richard had made with the Johnson boys. Still, he supposed if Peter was in the adventure, they could hardly keep Tony out. It was the whole idea he was unhappy about, but he had not the courage to say so. It was for this reason that he had remained silent, apart from his one protest to Richard, as Richard and Tony talked the matter over and made the final arrangements. Finally Richard turned to him and said, "Now Paul, will you take the first hour till the clock strikes nine and then wake me. Are you ready to settle down, Tony? You should have been asleep long ago, specially if you are coming with us later."

Tony had been busy climbing out of his pyjamas, putting on his underwear and shirt, and laying his sweater and shorts beside his sleeping bag. Then he climbed back into the bag, snuggled down and said, sleepily, "I'm glad I've not got to stay awake." Almost immediately he dropped asleep.

Richard lay awake for quite a long time, much to his annoyance. He kept telling himself that he must get to sleep quickly, as he only had till nine o'clock, but the more he thought about it, the more wide awake he felt. This seemed to go on for nearly an hour and he quite expected to hear the clock strike nine, but in reality he was sound asleep in a quarter of an hour.

Paul sat up in his sleeping bag at first, to keep himself awake, but after a time he became uncomfortable and stretched himself out, leaning on one elbow. Gradually his head dropped on to his arm and then he too slept.

CHAPTER VIII

SMUGGLERS' CAVE

PAUL woke with a start, stiff and cold from lying half out of his sleeping bag. For a moment he could not think, why he should be like that, until, to his horror, he realised that he had promised to stay awake until nine o'clock and then wake Richard. Whatever time must it be now? He lifted the side of the tent cautiously and looked across at the big tent, and saw to his relief that there was still a light showing. He lay down again, wondering whether he should wake Richard straight away, but he did not have to make up his mind because just at that moment he heard the church clock begin to strike. He counted the strokes carefully—one, two, three . . . eight, nine, ten. He rolled over felt in the dark for Richard's shoulder and shook it gently.

Richard woke immediately and seemed to know what was expected of him...

"All right, I'm awake. Is it time?" he asked in a whisper.

"Richard," whispered Paul in reply, "I'm afraid I went to sleep too, but I woke just before it struck ten, and there's still a light in the big tent."

"Oh, all right," said Richard. "All the better—now we've both had a sleep. I wonder if I ought to leave Tony to sleep.

"I don't see how you can now. You did promise and you know what a fuss he'd make, and probably let it all out if he discovered you'd been without him. Anyway, it's a bit hard, if Peter comes, to leave Tony out. I wish you'd never mentioned it to him, but now you have, you'll have to go through with it."

34

"I suppose you're right," said Richard, leaning over to the other side of the tent where Tony lay. He shook him gently, preparing to put his hand over his mouth if he protested loudly at being woken. His caution was not necessary, however, and Tony, after blinking owlishly a few times, climbed out of the sleeping bag and began to struggle into his clothes.

When the three boys were almost ready, Paul lifted the side again, just in time to see the light in the big tent go out.

"Light's just out," he whispered to Richard. "We needn't wait long now."

A few minutes later the three boys slid under the brailing at the far side of the tent, tiptoed across the field to a hole in the hedge, squeezed through it one after the other and set off along the cliff path towards Smugglers' Cove. They were armed with spades, which Richard had hidden in the hedge before he went to bed, and with flashlights. The latter were quite unnecessary, as the moon was up and nearly full. But though it gave a very bright light, it also cast a lot of shadows and made everywhere look quite different and rather eerie. Tony shivered and said under his breath, as if to himself, "Coo, I'm glad I'm not out here alone," and though the two older boys said nothing, they rather agreed with Tony.

Richard had been right when he said that no one would be about. They did not see a single person all the way to Smugglers' Cove, though there was a light showing from the window of the beachmaster's cottage which they could see from the path above the Cove. When they reached the bottom of the steps, out of sight of the cottage, they felt quite safe from fear of detection, and sat down to wait for Colin and Peter.

The minutes seemed to drag like hours as they waited; once they jumped up on hearing footsteps, but they belonged to someone walking past the Cove along the path, and no one came down the steps.

Finally, when they were all getting very cold from sitting on the stone steps, Richard turned to the others.

"I say, this is no joke. I vote we start digging to find a way in and that will keep us warm, and we'll be all ready when Colin and Peter come. Where do you think we should start?"

"Well," said Paul, "if it really is a tunnel, I expect it would start pretty low down, don't you? After all, if they had to take the things they smuggled in that way, they couldn't take anything very heavy high up, could they? What about looking round about where we are now?"

"Good idea!" said Tony, peering under the step on which he was sitting, the second from the bottom. "Look here, there's a bit of a gap here."

"Not big enough," said Richard. "We can't stay here too long, you know, and we must find the biggest gap there is so there'll be less digging."

They soon decided on the biggest gap and started to dig, stopping every few moments to make sure no-one was watching, and to look for the Johnson boys. After ten minutes, the whole was large enough to take Tony, and by shining their torches they could see that the gap continued upwards further than the beams of torchlight went. The three boys gasped at the sight and then Richard took charge.

"Now then, the question is, shall we go on digging to make the gap bigger, in the hope that the Johnsons will turn up soon, or do we send Tony up to see if it leads anywhere before we dig any further?"

"Do you think the Johnsons will be coming now?" asked Paul.

"Course they won't," said Tony eagerly. "Let me go in and have a look for you. I've got my spaceman's torch here."

"What do you say, Paul?" asked Richard.

"Well it does seem pointless to spend more time digging if it doesn't lead anywhere, doesn't it? And I don't think we can wait any longer for the Johnsons, do you?"

"All right then, Tony. In you go! Gently does it!" commanded Richard.

Tony climbed into the hole they had dug, got on his hands and knees and began to climb up under the steps, calling out every few seconds, "Coo, it's cold under here," "There's not much room," "I'm glad I've got my supersonic torch." His voice sounded very muffled to the two boys, but it continued until, as far as they could tell, he had climbed about halfway up. Then suddenly there was a stifled cry of terror followed by complete silence.

The two older boys stared at each other in horror for a second and then almost simultaneously dropped on their hands and knees, calling, "What's the matter, Tony? Are you all right?"

The seconds seemed endless to the frightened boys, before they heard Tony's voice, even fainter and more muffled than it had been before, calling, "Oh help! I'm stuck. I can't move either up or down and my mouth's full of sand and I can hardly breathe."

"Whatever happened, Tony, and whereabouts are you? Don't panic. We'll dig you out in no time." It was Paul who had taken command. Richard seemed to be unable to think of any practical action to take. The thought which came back to him again and again was, "What will Daddy and Mummy say if anything happens to Tony? It's all my fault. I'm responsible."

Tony replied in that frightening, faint voice, "I stepped on a bank of sand and it gave way and I went down with it. Do think of something quickly you two!"

Again Paul spoke, quietly and reassuringly, "Look, Tony,

can you work your hand out—your right hand, the one you write with—through the sand so that we know exactly where you are and we won't waste a lot of time digging in the wrong place."

They could hear the sound of Tony panting and it was obviously a great effort for him even to push his hand out, but at last it appeared about a yard below where they were watching. They snatched up their spades and began to dig feverishly, removing the sand around Tony's arm until they reached his armpit. Then they were in a dilemma as they realised that his head was alongside one of the wide pillars that supported the steps and that they could not dig straight towards it to reach him and give him the air he so much needed. It was then that they first realised too that it would take them a very long time, just the two of them digging with their small spades, to release Tony, and Paul said to Richard quickly, "Look, we must have help. We don't know how long Tony can last there, specially as we can't get near his head to give him air. Is there anyone near we can get at quickly?"

Richard's wits were coming back to him and he replied immediately, "Yes, the beachmaster's house is just up near the top there. He's the best person, and you know we saw a light as we passed. Shall I go and fetch him?"

"Yes, you know the way and will get there quicker than I can. But do be quick and I'll keep on digging."

When Richard had disappeared up the steps Paul stopped digging for a minute and, leaning down, called, "Tony, can you hear me? Are you all right? Richard's gone to fetch the beachmaster, so we'll have you out in no time."

Tony's reply was even fainter than it had been before. "Do hurry up. I'm passing out under here."

Paul was a little reassured by this. He thought that Tony would not speak like that if he really were passing out.

Nevertheless, he went on digging desperately, and was dismayed at the little headway he seemed to be making. As he dug, all kinds of frightening and bitter thoughts chased round and round in his mind.

"Suppose the beachmaster isn't in. Suppose he's in bed and Richard can't wake him. What if Tony isn't getting enough air? He won't last long. Why ever did I give in to Richard? Sheer cowardice, that's what it was. And I'd resolved to do nothing to displease Mr. and Mrs. Challenger or be a bad example to the others. Fancy letting Richard bring Tony on a wildgoose chase like this! Fancy agreeing to come at all!" And the more he thought of it all, the more he blamed himself.

The time Richard was away seemed to be going on for ever, but at last he heard his voice at the top of the cliff saying, "There, just down there." Paul, as he looked up, saw him leading the way, followed by a big, kind-looking man, with white hair, who was carrying a large spade, a thermos flask and a blanket.

"Well, now, where is the youngster?" he asked.

"There's his arm, sir," answered Paul. "And I've dug quite a bit away from him but you see I can't get the sand away from his head because of the pillar. My spade's not long enough to reach. He's still all right. He was talking to me just now."

"All right, don't worry. I'll soon have him out with this big spade. First of all, let's see if I can get him some air."

As he spoke, the beachmaster drove the spade in gently alongside the pillar, well under the place where Tony's head was lying, and as he drew out a spadeful of sand, the children heard Tony saying, with relief, "Coo, that's better!"

After that the beachmaster, with quick firm digging, each spadeful removing three or four times the amount Richard and Paul could do with theirs, soon cleared enough of the sand away to be able to grasp Tony by the waist and to drag him gently from under the steps.

"Coo!" said Tony again, as soon as he was out, and then quite suddenly he seemed to crumple up, and began to whimper.

"Steady now, son, you're quite all right. Here, take a drink of this. It's only water but it keeps nice and cold in a thermos. I always keep a thermos full of fresh water by me for people like you."

He went on talking reassuringly, and as he talked he wrapped a blanket round Tony, and gradually the colour came back into his cheeks. When he decided that Tony had recovered sufficiently to be taken home he turned to the others and said, "You two boys feel all right? Now, where do you live, or where are you staying?"

"We're camping in the field belonging to Limekiln Farm, on the other side of the cliff path, sir," answered Richard.

"All right then, you lead the way and I'll carry this young man. What's your name, son?" he asked Tony.

"Tony Challenger, sir," replied Tony. "I'm all right now. I can walk."

"Well, you're not going to try whether you can or not. I expect you'd find your knees a bit wobbly if you did. Now, while we're going along, tell me whatever you boys were doing to get Tony stuck like that."

Tony told the whole tale and when he had finished the beachmaster laughed softly.

"Well, well! You boys will never learn, will you? I know every nook and cranny of these cliffs and there's no secret cave round here, though it is still called Smuggler's Cove. Well, I expect it's taught you a lesson, that's one thing."

CHAPTER IX

THE CONSEQUENCES

THE two older boys plodded ahead in silence. Both of them were wondering what their reception would be when they got back to camp. What would Mr. Challenger say? The journey seemed all too short and it was two very frightened boys who led the way into the field towards Mr. and Mrs. Challenger's big tent.

The beachmaster banged on the door of the tent and after a moment Mr. Challenger appeared, wearing his pyjamas and with a coat flung over his shoulders.

"Sorry to bother you, sir. These boys were in a spot of trouble and came to me for help. The young one has had a bit of a shaking-up. Perhaps he'd be better with a hot drink before he goes back to bed."

Mr. Challenger took Tony in his arms and in a moment Mrs. Challenger had come out, also with a coat over her nightclothes.

"Would you like to sleep in with us tonight, Tony?" she asked. "Daddy can bring your sleeping bag in here while I get a drink."

"Yes please, Mummy," said a very subdued Tony.

"What about you two? Do you want a drink too?" she asked.

"No thank you," they replied.

"All right then. Cut along to bed now. We'll have all explanations in the morning," said Mr. Challenger. "I'll come and fetch Tony's things."

He sat Tony down inside the big tent and went with the

two boys while Mrs. Challenger busied herself at the side of the tent with the primus stove and spoke in low tones to the beachmaster.

"What were they up to?" she asked.

"Well, Ma'am, they had some wild idea about the Smuggler's Cove and thought there must be a passage under the steps. They sent young Tony in and he got stuck. They had the sense to come to me pretty quickly for help, but I don't think the lad would have stayed conscious much longer."

"Thank you very much indeed for helping. I'm only sorry you've had the trouble. We had no idea at all that they were out."

"Tony did say something about arranging to meet some friends, but that they had not turned up."

At this point Mr. Challenger returned with Tony's sleeping bag and pyjamas under his arm.

"I hope my wife has been telling you how grateful we are for the trouble you've taken."

"Oh, that's all right, sir. It's part of my job. If I can have my blanket I'll be off now. Send the lads up in the morning to tell me that they're all right, especially young Tony. He has plenty of pluck."

"All right, I will. I'll just fetch your blanket."

Mr. Challenger disappeared into the tent, spread Tony's sleeping bag out alongside where he was sitting, handed him his pyjamas and said, "There you are son. Hop on to your sleeping bag and get into your pyjamas quickly. Give me the blanket so that I can give it back to the beachmaster before he goes."

"Daddy," said Tony hesitantly, "he was awfully decent to me. Will you say 'thank you' for me?"

"Of course I will. I'm glad you thought of it." said Mr. Challenger and he went out reflecting that the fright had done Tony no harm; it was not often he was thoughtful about such details.

"Here's your blanket back, thank you very much. Tony specially asked me to say 'thank you' too."

"Very glad to do anything to help, sir."

"By the way," added Mr. Challenger, "have you seen any suspicious characters round here at all? We've missed one or two things, and the latest we cannot afford to lose; some of our spare blankets."

"Why no sir, I've seen no-one, though I did hear that some campers on a site towards Penton had lost quite a few things. Did you tell the police?"

"Well no, I rather thought I'd wait to see if there were further developments, and meanwhile keep my eyes open."

"Yes, well, that's your affair, sir, though I think I'd be inclined to report it. That sort of thing ought to be nipped in the bud before it goes further, don't you think, sir?"

"Hm. I'll have to think about it. Anyway, thank you again for all your trouble."

"No trouble, sir. Goodnight to you both."

He disappeared along the path and Mrs. Challenger carried the hot drink she had prepared into the tent, followed by her husband. Tony was already in his sleeping bag, sitting up, and he took the drink gratefully.

"You'd better have these too, Tony. They'll send you off to sleep all the quicker," said Mrs. Challenger, handing him two junior aspirins. He took them and very quickly disposed of them and the drink and lay down, murmuring sleepily, "Thanks ever so, Mummy."

Richard and Paul hardly talked at all as they undressed and got into bed, but just before they dropped off to sleep Paul said, "I say Richard, your father wasn't a bit angry, was he?"

Richard replied thoughtfully, "No, he's hardly ever angry,

but he can make you feel ever so small when he tells you off. You wait till the morning."

And with this comforting thought they both settled down to sleep. Suddenly, Paul sat up.

"Richard," he exclaimed in a whisper, "did you notice anything as we came through the gate with the beach-master? I'd forgotten all about it till this minute."

"Why, yes, I'd forgotten too. I saw someone getting through the hole in the hedge, the way we went tonight. Only I was too worried wondering what Daddy and Mummy would say to bother much."

"Same here. Who could it be? Couldn't have been a grown-up, could it? That hole's not big enough. Did you notice if there was just one or more? You were ahead of me."

"I think I saw two, but I couldn't be very sure. It wasn't light enough."

"Oh well," said Paul, sleepily, "it's no good worrying now. There's nothing we can do if they've pinched anything else and they're not likely to come back tonight after being disturbed once. Let's get to sleep."

Paul went out first to wash the next morning and on his way he was met by Mr. Challenger, who said straight away, "Now look here, Paul, I think you boys had enough of a fright last night to have learnt your lesson and I'm not going to say any more about it. But one thing we must have clear. I'm responsible to your aunt for you, and I think you'll admit you can do pretty much what you please during the day, but I must know where you are at night. That's understood, isn't it?"

Mr. Challenger spoke so kindly that Paul suddenly felt overwhelmed by what he described to himself as Mr. Challenger's decency, and he suddenly wanted to cry. Whatever happened he must not do that! He hastily muttered, "Yes, of course, Mr. Challenger. I—I'm awfully sorry."

His voice was so gruff that he sounded sulky, but Mr. Challenger seemed to understand and said with a smile, "That's all right, Paul. Now hurry up with that washing or there'll be a queue behind you."

Mr. Challenger had more to say to Richard. After making the rule about not going out at night that he had made to Paul, he added, "I'm disappointed in you, Richard. I thought you hoped that as a result of camping with us here and what he hears at the beach services, Paul would be persuaded to become a Christian. You've not gone the best way to help him, have you? I don't know whose idea it all was but, as a Christian, you shouldn't have been in on it at all, should you?"

Richard was appalled. He realised of course that he had behaved badly but it had never occurred to him that this might stop Paul from becoming a Christian, which was the thing he wanted almost more than anything else, at present. He so hoped that one of the results of the holiday would be that he and Paul might go together as Christians to their new school. And to make matters worse was that the expedition had been all his idea, even the original arrangement with the Johnsons, and now he must tell his father. He looked very ashamed as he said in a low voice, "It's worse than you think, Daddy. It was all my idea and Paul did say we oughtn't to and I laughed at him. I honestly never thought it would make any difference to Paul becoming a Christian. What ought I to do?"

"Well, Richard, what do you think you ought to do?"

Richard thought hard for a minute. He could only think of one solution but he hated the idea. But finally, after a struggle in his mind, he turned to his father.

"I suppose I could make it right with Paul, couldn't I, Daddy? Apologise, I mean, for laughing at him and for suggesting it all."

"I think that's the right thing, yes, and perhaps you'll get a chance to tell Paul that you are a Christian. That might help a bit, mightn't it?"

Richard wondered about that. Surely this would be just the wrong time to make a lot about being a Christian when he had not behaved a bit like one and had got Paul into trouble into the bargain. However, he did not mention his doubts to his father, who left the tent saying, "Well, anyway, see how things work out. And don't be late for breakfast."

He waited nervously till Paul came back from washing and then said to him slowly, "I say, Paul, I think I ought to 'apol'."

To his surprise, Paul looked completely mystified.

"To 'apol'? Why, whatever do you mean?" he asked.

Richard laughed and suddenly felt a little better.

"What an idiot I am! 'Apol' is short for 'apologise' in our family, and when we have to say 'sorry' about anything it somehow seems easier to say 'apol'! Anyway, I am sorry about last night. It was all my fault and it was mean to laugh at you when you said we oughtn't to go. And anyway, you were right and I was wrong."

"Well, your father was most frightfully decent about it all. Listen, Richard, I know you said he could make you feel small when he told you off, but isn't he ever mad about things? I know when I do anything wrong at home Auntie loses her temper and lets fly. I can't remember what Daddy and Mummy used to do, though."

Richard thought for a moment and then tried to explain.

"Daddy talked to me about it once. He said that, of course, if we're naughty we have to be punished or told off, but if you're a Christian you shouldn't lose your temper about it. And he said that he and Mummy always try not to be cross however naughty we are. He said that God never is, when we sin, because He wants to forgive us, and they try not to be, too."

Richard hesitated and then went on again boldly, not wanting to lose the opportunity his father had said might come.

"And Paul, I know you might not think so after last night, but I'm a Christian, too, and I hope I shall grow up to be like Mummy and Daddy."

Paul said nothing for a moment and Richard thought he had offended him and just then they heard Mr. Challenger's voice calling, "Breakfast up!" Richard hastily ran a comb through his hair and said to Paul, "I've not washed—I'll have to do it after!" and Paul grinned and said, "If you do at all!" and then added quickly, "Thanks ever so much for telling me about your parents and about being a Christian."

And the two boys ran across to where breakfast was laid out and settled down to enjoy it with the others. Tony, apparently quite recovered from the night's adventure, grinned at them both as they sat down.

CHAPTER X

THE MISSING BATHING THINGS

THE two boys learned later in the day that Colin had had a bilious attack during the previous evening and had been taken to sleep indoors. Naturally he had told Peter that he was not to go down to the beach by himself. Peter, when he heard all that had happened, was secretly rather glad he had not been there. But by the time Richard and Paul heard all this something else had happened at the camp that seemed to them much more important.

The children went to collect their bathing costumes and towels before setting off for the beach service. Anne came back from the line, calling, "Mummy, have you moved Richard's and my bathing things? Our costumes aren't there, and there are two towels short, too."

Mrs. Challenger came out of her tent and said, "No, Anne, I've not touched them. Are you quite sure you hung them up yesterday?"

"Oh yes, Mummy," said Richard who had joined them. "I remember we all put them up at dinner time after we'd used them in the morning."

"Well," asked Mr. Challenger, "did anyone notice if they were still there at bedtime? I can't say I did myself."

No-one could remember going near the line after tea, and then suddenly Paul and Richard remembered, both at the same moment, the intruders they had seen the previous night.

"Daddy!" exclaimed Richard.

"Oh, Mr. Challenger!" cried Paul at the same time, and they both stopped and looked at each other.

"Go on, you tell him, Richard," said Paul.

"Well, Daddy, we forgot all about it, but when we were coming in at the gate last night with the beachmaster, Paul and I saw two people disappearing through that hole in the hedge. They can't have been very big 'cos that hole's only just big enough for me."

"And they've taken our costumes and not yours and Mummy's," said Anne, "so that means they must have been children."

"But who would want to do a thing like that? And what parents would let their children out at that time? And what would they want with bathing costumes? I'd thought of the other thefts as by grown-ups. Surely it's not children who had all those blankets?" Mrs. Challenger looked very puzzled.

"They were not the only children out late last night anyway," said Mr. Challenger, with a look at the boys, who all grew rather red. "But that's by the way. I think, after this, I ought to go to the police, though I'm even less anxious to do it if the culprits are children."

"Well, after all," said Mrs. Challenger, "we don't know that the two that Richard and Paul saw are the ones who did the stealing. And we can't just let it go on, can we?"

"No, you're right, we can't. You children had better cut along to the beach or you'll find all the pulpit-digging done. And I'll call at the police station before I come down."

Mrs. Challenger said, "Richard, you and Anne will find your old costumes in the black case in my tent. I brought them as spares in case we couldn't get our things dry at any time. You'll find some towels there too."

At dinner that day Mr. Challenger told them that he had heard from the local police sergeant, that there had been several other thefts reported.

"They are all from campers, it seems, and the odd thing is the thefts are nearly all food or children's clothes."

"Do you mean that children are doing all the stealing, Daddy?" asked Anne.

"I'm not definitely saying that, Anne, but it looks a bit like it. Though I can't quite imagine why, or what the parents are up to. They surely must realise the things are stolen when the children bring them home. However, that's enough of that for the moment. What's the programme this afternoon?"

"Water-games for inters. and juniors, Daddy, as it's so hot. Should be super!" said Tony.

"All right, Tony. Have a good time but don't go playing any tricks, will you?"

"No, Daddy. Come on you lot!" and off they raced. The games that afternoon were great fun and quite the best thing to do on such a hot afternoon. The intermediates played water halo and leap-frog, but their object was to keep as cool as they could. Paul noticed Hans and Gerda and realised that he had not seen them in any of the organised swims before.

"Oh well," he thought, "perhaps they are not very keen on bathing usually. But when it is as hot as this it's the only thing worth doing."

Hans was drying quite close to them when the games were over, and Paul noticed Richard watching him rather closely. Hans suddenly noticed Richard's interest and seemed to redden and immediately picked up the rest of his clothes and wandered off along the beach, putting them on as he went, not waiting for Gerda.

"I say, Richard," said Paul, "what's bitten you?"

"Didn't you notice, Paul?" replied Richard. "No, you probably wouldn't, but I'm positive that towel Hans was using was one of the ones that went off our line last night."

"Oh, stuff!" retorted Paul. "What would Hans want it for?"

"That's what I can't make out, either. Surely his mother would give him a towel for bathing. But listen, have you ever noticed the twins bathing before?"

"That's funny! I was just thinking earlier on it was the first time they'd been in. But Richard, what about the trunks? Were those yours?"

"Can't tell," said Richard, shaking his head. "Could be. They're just ordinary black ones, but they might belong to anyone. Lots of boys had ones like that on today. We both had, for instance, hadn't we?"

"Mm. I suppose so. What are you going to do? Tell your father?"

"No, not just yet. It seems a bit mean on the twins. Let's investigate a bit for ourselves."

"How?" queried Paul.

"I don't quite know. I wondered if we could trail them some time and see where they lived. That might help, mightn't it?"

So they agreed to watch for an opportunity to do just that, and meanwhile not to mention the matter to anyone else.

"It's an awful shame," sighed Paul. "I rather like them, especially after the games this afternoon. And did you see those wonderful leap-frogs Hans was doing?"

CHAPTER XI

MISSIONARY DAY

THE rest of the week went by all too quickly for the children. Something fresh was arranged for each afternoon. Thursday was missionary day so there was also something special in the morning.

The speaker was a missionary from the Near East and he was dressed as an Eastern Shepherd. He described to them the work of these shepherds as he had seen it carried out in the countries he had come from, and he gave the children a very clear picture of the Lord Jesus as the Good Shepherd. He ended by making them learn the verse from John, chapter ten: 'I am the Good Shepherd: the Good Shepherd giveth his life for the sheep', and went on to describe how, even in modern times, shepherds in the East had to protect themselves from wild beasts and it was still possible for them to lose their lives in protecting their sheep.

Paul, although he had listened to most of the talk with interest, found his thoughts wandering just at the end, and he began to wonder just what all this meant to him. He knew that Christ had died for the sins of the world, and though he had not thought the matter out carefully, he had always assumed that because of that everything was all right. Then Mr. Johnson's words of last Sunday came back to him: "It's something that no-one else can do for you; you have to decide for yourself if you will accept what the Lord Jesus did for you. And you know, if you don't accept and say 'Thank you', it's just the same as saying, 'I don't want it!' "

Paul began to realise that all that he had been hearing

since Sunday did after all matter to him, and just as he came to this conclusion the talk ended and he dismissed the matter again from his mind for the time being.

On Thursday afternoon there was a sand-modelling competition in one of the larger coves where there was plenty of sand. The children worked in groups of six, made up of some from each age group. They had to make models which had some connection with life overseas, and the missionary speaker of the morning was to judge the results. The Challenger family and Paul, with Pauline Johnson to make up their number, worked together and made a model of an African village. They had planned it all at lunch time, and on their way to the beach had gathered some things they needed, such as long pieces of coarse grass to make thatch for the huts, an old sand bucket and sticks and string to make a well, stones to build an open fireplace in the centre of the village, and various other things which they thought might be useful. Another group had made a model of the Taj Mahal, a tomb in India, which is said to be the most beautiful in the world. The group in which the rest of the Johnson children were had chosen the Egyptian Pyramid and Sphinx, and another group modelled a map of North and South America in relief. In fact there were so many good ideas, and the standard of the models was so high, that the missionary found it hard to choose the best. Finally he decided to give the first prize to the Taj Mahal, the second to the Challengers' African village, and the third prize to the map of America.

After the competition was over, they all gathered together to eat a picnic tea and when they had finished they listened to several exciting stories told by the missionary. As they broke up to go home, Mr. Johnson said, "Now don't forget that the prizes will be distributed after the beach service tomorrow morning, so mind you come!"

The next morning there was the excitement of receiving their prizes after the beach service. The custom was that each boy had to drop a curtsy and each girl had to make a bow, up on the sand pulpit in front of all the other children, before the prizes were actually handed to them. The boys complained afterwards that it was much harder for them, but, of course, the girls did not agree. They did not discuss the matter for long, however; they were too busy examining the beautiful books they had been given. Whoever had chosen the prizes seemed to know exactly what each of them liked, and they were all satisfied.

CHAPTER XII

THE GOBLIN'S REVENGE

FRIDAY afternoon was one of adventure for Elizabeth, and for Tony, who also chose to go with the tiny tots. When they met as usual by the harbour wall, they were told that Miss Conway had been captured by the wicked goblin whose store of chocolate they had found on Tuesday afternoon. A letter in very queer handwriting had been pushed through the letterbox just before dinner, even before anyone had missed Miss Conway. The workers were quite unable to decipher what the letter said until suddenly one of them suggested that it might be mirror hand-writing and, sure enough, when they held it in front of the mirror, the writing became quite clear. This is what it said:

'Your worker will be fed on bread and water and made to knit socks for me to make up for the chocolate you stole. It will be no use looking for her. I have hidden her where you will not find her.'

"And now," said Mr. Collier, "it's our job to rescue Miss Conway."

"But how can we? He said we'd never find her," objected one of the children.

"Ah well, as a matter of fact we have a clue," said Mr. Collier mysteriously, and he held up a dried pea. "I found this outside our house, and several others too. Now, that means that he still has some of the peas he used the other day to make a trail to his treasure. It also means that he must have a hole in his pocket, so we have to start again to follow his trail. But mind you, it won't be so easy this time because he obviously did not mean to leave a trail and there

55

will probably only be a pea now and again, so we need all your help."

And so they set off, as they had on Tuesday, only, as Mr. Collier had warned them, it was very much harder work. Some times there would not be anything for some yards, and then perhaps only one pea, which was not always easy to pick out. However, slowly they found a definite trail which led them towards the woods behind the village. When they got to the stile leading to the woods, Mr. Challenger stopped them.

"We'll have to follow very carefully now because the peas will be harder to see. And we'll have to look all round in case the goblin is hiding among the trees. He might try to capture one of us, so keep together because he'll never dare to attack so many of us."

They closed up and followed the path in a bunch but presently one very small girl began to cry. Miss Porter, a worker who had only arrived that morning, stopped and, kneeling down, put her arms round her and asked her what was the matter. At first the child was unable to answer and only cried all the more, but eventually she found her voice and sobbed, "I want to go back to Mummy. I'm frightened of the goblin."

Miss Porter sent the other children on with Mr. Collier. Some had laughed and looked rather superior when they heard what the little girl had said, obviously knowing that the goblin was not real. Tony nearly said out loud, "Don't be silly. It's not real," but he stopped himself just in time, remembering how, when he had discovered that Father Christmas was not a real person, Mummy had made him promise not to tell Elizabeth so that she could go on believing he was while she was still little. He realised that this was the same sort of thing and that some of the children there would be believing it all and it was not fair to spoil their fun.

When the others had all gone, Miss Porter said comfortingly to the little girl, "Darling, the goblin can't possibly hurt us because you see he is not real. Mr. Collier made him up. It's all pretend."

The child, whose name Miss Porter later discovered was Alison, looked up at her unbelievingly.

"Not real? But what happened to Miss Conway? And who put the peas there?"

Miss Porter explained, "Well, you see, the workers made the story up, and then sent Miss Conway away to hide and she dropped the peas as she went so that you should have the fun of following the trail and finding her."

Alison's face cleared a little and then clouded over again.

"What about the letter then? That was real. You showed it to us."

Miss Porter laughed. "Mr. Johnson wrote that. He's the only one of us who can do mirror writing! And now, what would you like to do? Would you still like to go back to Mummy or will you come on and catch the others up?"

Alison hesitated. She was obviously still rather frightened in spite of Miss Porter's reassurances.

"I think I'd like to go to Mummy. But you'll come with me till we're through the wood, won't you?"

"Of course I will. I'm coming all the way with you, don't worry! Do you know where Mummy will be?"

"Oh yes, she and Daddy will be in Smuggler's Cove with my baby brother."

"All right then, off we go!" said Miss Porter, and together they turned back along the path.

Meanwhile the rest of the children and Mr. Collier went on following the trail quietly, not talking above a whisper in case the goblin heard them, and presently they came to the end of the wood and turned out on to the road for a short way and then off the road again on to a footpath which led across a large field. The trail did not lead them along the footpath but across the field towards a large tree which stood in one corner. Suddenly one of the children, whose home was in Banstone and who knew it very well, said in a loud voice, "I know. She's in the hollow oak," and she started to run, followed by all the others. Sure enough, when they reached the other side of the tree, they saw Miss Conway sitting in the hollow space at the base of the tree tied by the arms to the tree with a piece of rope which was slack enough for her to get on with some knitting in red wool which she had in her hands. By her side was a bottle of water and a chunk of rather dry looking bread.

She looked up as she heard them coming and cried, "Oh, I'm so glad someone's come to rescue me. I thought I should have to stay here all night!"

The children crowded round, all asking questions, while two of them cut the rope with Mr. Collier's knife. Miss Conway told them how she had been attacked from behind in the lane at the back of the Mission House, blindfolded and dragged a long way; then she was told to sit down, tied up and told to get on with the knitting or else! She did not know who had done it because the bandage was not removed from her eyes until she had been told what to do and had discovered the knitting and the bread and water beside her.

Elizabeth was full of this adventure when she and Tony got back to the camp. She told her parents the whole story.

"And Mummy," she ended, "Alison was frightened of the goblin and went back to her Mummy."

"Oh, and weren't you frightened?" asked Mrs. Challenger, smiling.

"Of course not, Mummy. The goblin would never have come near us. Mr. Collier was there."

Tony waited until Elizabeth was looking the other way; then he grinned at his mother and gave her a slow wink.

CHAPTER XIII

WEEK'S END

FRIDAY was the last day of the week as far as the mission activities were concerned. The workers had a rest on Saturdays and the children were left to look after themselves.

It was on Friday afternoon that Richard and Paul found an opportunity to follow Hans and Gerda. The afternoon games had finished early and Hans and Gerda, as usual, went along the beach in the opposite direction from most of the other children. Richard, watching them go, nudged Paul.

"What about it now, Paul? We've plenty of time before tea and we might be able to keep an eye on them if we take to the rocks and keep almost on a level with them on the beach. Looks as if they're going that way and the tide's out. They won't have to go up on the rocks at all."

"All right, but we'll have to hurry to get level with them in the first place."

They set off at a good pace, keeping close to the rocks, and climbing over them when Hans' and Gerda's path came too close. They very soon were level with the twins and could go a little more slowly and get their breath. Hans and Gerda did not seem to have noticed them, or to have any suspicion that they were being followed. They kept to the beach, in the direction of Penton, and then, quite suddenly, they turned sharply towards the rocks. Richard and Paul, fortunately for them, were at a point where the rocks were very broken up and there were several little inlets, almost as big as caves, just behind them. Paul seized Richard by the arm and pulled him down and then, almost crawling, they scrambled as fast as they could into one of the caves. They crouched down, trying hard not to breathe too loud, for what seemed a very long minute. Then Richard edged out, keeping down, and put his head round the edge of a boulder to investigate.

"I say, Paul," he half whispered, half said out loud, "there's not a sign of them."

Paul came out too and together they searched for a few moments in all the inlets in that particular stretch of rocks.

"We seem to have lost them, but I can't think where," murmured Paul. "And I think we'll have to leave it at that, don't you? It must be pretty nearly teatime by now."

"Yes, I suppose so," returned Richard. "It's a pity when we seemed to be on their track."

They returned and made their way back to the camp arriving just in time for tea.

On Friday evening there was a special event for which all the children were allowed to stay up. A sausage sizzle was held up on the cliff top for all ages, and the Challenger party arrived at seven o'clock to find a big, glowing fire, and Mrs. Johnson and several other workers crouched over it, cooking sausages on a grid that had been placed over the fire. The children had each brought bread to eat with the sausages, but some of them preferred to find sticks to use as forks and eat the sausages by themselves. When there were no more left, they were all allowed to gather round and cook anything else they had brought. The favourite was potatoes in their jackets, and though these usually ended up black on the outside and raw in the middle and to the grown-ups looked most indigestible, the children thought they were wonderful and certainly none of them had tummyache after eating them!

When they had all had their fill and it was beginning to get dark, Mr. Johnson gathered them round the fire which had by now died down to a mass of red embers. They settled down to a quarter of an hour's sing-song of some of the camp-fire favourites before they were packed off home. Many of the parents came up to take their children home, and they left Mr. Johnson and some other workers clearing away the last of the fire, putting back the turf and leaving everything as they had found it in true Scout fashion.

After breakfast on Saturday morning, which was later than usual because they had been late the night before, Mr. Challenger said, "What does everyone think about a picnic today? We could take the car and have lunch somewhere near Penny Falls and then go on to see Little Naples in the afternoon."

"Oo, ye-es!" chorused the children, all except Paul who did not know either place, and felt in any case that he ought to fit in with any plans that were made.

Richard turned to him. "They're both smashing places, Paul, so you say 'yes' too. I'll tell you all about them."

"Why, of course," said Paul, a little embarrassed at being asked his opinion. "That'll be grand!"

The children rushed about, trying to do their chores in specially quick time, while Mrs. Challenger prepared the picnic lunch and tea. She and Mr. Challenger seemed to have had the matter well planned beforehand, because the children noticed that she happened to have in the store tent just the things they needed for a picnic, and everything was soon ready.

As they drove towards Penny Falls, the four older children squashed in the back and Elizabeth on Mrs. Challenger's knee in the front, Richard explained to Paul why the Falls had such an unusual name. There were pebbles of a special kind at the bottom of the falls and the water, as it fell from a great height, made them jingle like a lot of copper coins, and that was why everyone called them Penny Falls. Although there was an official name, no-one seemed to know what it was.

"And there are some wizard rocks up the side which Daddy lets us climb," added Tony. This part was the most exciting for him. The previous year he had not managed to climb very high and he was hoping to do better this year.

Richard then went on to describe Little Naples, which was a village built in Italian style.

"All the houses are like they are in Italy, and there are lots of little pools and waterfalls, and the woods round about are made up of Mediterranean shrubs and trees. There are some lovely long tunnels, with trees meeting right over the top, and it's a smashing place for hide-and-seek."

The whole day was a great success. They had lunch in a shady spot near Penny Falls, after visiting the falls and having a try at climbing the rocks. Lunch was not a sandwich meal—the Challenger family scorned sandwiches and believed in picnicking in style. They had pork pie, lettuce, tomato, grated cheese, and potato mayonnaise, and for a second course there was a ripe juicy pear for each of them.

The visit to Little Naples pleased them all, particularly Paul, who had never seen such an interesting place before. After looking round the village, they played hide-and-seek in the woods, and then went down to the beach and bathed before tea to cool themselves.

They arrived back in camp rather exhausted and, for once, none of them objected when the time came to go to bed.

CHAPTER XIV

PAUL'S DECISION

PAUL, remembering the previous Sunday, was not expecting to enjoy this one. There had been so much religion—family prayers after breakfast, church in the morning, family beach service, and then possibly some of them would go to church in the evening.

Paul had begun to enjoy family prayers, now he was getting used to them, and the family beach service would probably be very similar to the morning services they had had all the week. It was church that he found difficult. It did not seem to be meant for him in the same way as the other things did. What a pity it was that the church at Banstone had no special 'children's church' as Richard told him they had at their church at home!

As he sat in church, Paul thought a lot about his past weeks with the Challenger family. He thought again of how different they were from other families he had had anything to do with. Was it because of family prayers? Or was it because they were Christians as Richard had told him? And if so, what did that mean and how was it connected with what he had been hearing at the beach services during the week? What he really needed was to talk it over with someone and he supposed Mr. Challenger was the obvious person, but somehow he did not like the idea of approaching him.

The matter was solved for him, however, because after the service on the beach he found himself walking along the path towards camp with Mr. Challenger. As it happened, Mr. Challenger had been the speaker that afternoon and it seemed natural that the conversation should turn to something he had said which puzzled Paul.

"Mr. Challenger," he said, rather diffidently, but not feeling nearly so shy about it as he would have expected, "what did you mean in your talk when you said to the parents, 'It's not enough to bring your children up well, and then send them or take them to church—that won't make them or you into Christians, and won't build up a Christian family either'? Richard told me that you were Christians, and isn't that just what you do?"

"Yes, of course, Paul, but there's more to it than that. We don't claim to be any better than other people, don't think that. But you know, being a Christian isn't just doing things. Do you remember the first time it mentions Christians in the Bible? It says in Acts that 'The disciples were called Christians first in Antioch', and it describes those disciples as those who had 'believed and turned to the Lord'. You see, it didn't seem to depend on what they did, so much as on their believing in the Lord Jesus Christ and following Him."

"Yes, but," objected Paul, "surely everyone believes in Him now—in our country anyway."

"Do they, Paul?" asked Mr. Challenger quietly. "Do you, for instance?"

"Me! Why, of course I do!" Paul was shocked and a little indignant that Mr. Challenger should think he did not. He was not like the heathen people the missionary had talked about on Wednesday!

"Well, think of all that's involved before you're so positive. First of all, why did Jesus die? After all, He was God's Son and could do what He pleased, couldn't He?"

"For people's sins, didn't He?" suggested Paul, hesitantly. "To forgive them, I mean."

"Quite right," replied Mr. Challenger. "But you know,

we have to be more definite than that. 'People' means us—
you and me. I've got to admit and you've got to admit that
we ourselves are sinners and need forgiving. There's a
verse in Isaiah which says, 'All our righteousnesses are as
filthy rags'. In other words, even the very best we can do—
living good lives, going to church, etc.—is no use to God
until we have asked Him to forgive us. And admitting to
God that we are sinners must come before anything else.
So you see, there's an awful lot more than you'd think at
first involved in this matter of believing."

"Well then, what did Mr. Johnson mean last Sunday
when he said about not accepting being as bad as refusing?"

"Well, suppose I offered you a brand new bicycle and you
just looked at it and shrugged your shoulders and said to
yourself, 'I suppose he is offering it to me, but, after all,
why bother?' That would be worse than refusing, wouldn't
it? Yet, so many people are like that nowadays. They believe in a vague sort of way that the Lord Jesus died for the
sins of the world, but they shrug their shoulders and say to
themselves, 'Yes, I suppose that's true, but what has it to do
with me? I'm quite all right as I am. I don't need to be
forgiven'. They won't believe the most important part—
that they are sinners themselves and need Him to forgive
them."

"Yes, I suppose so," said Paul thoughtfully. He was beginning to realise that this was just what he had been doing.
"Then, what exactly is becoming a Christian?"

"Simply admitting to God that you are a sinner and asking
Him to forgive your sin and take it away, because of what the
Lord Jesus Christ has done. In other words, as Mr. Johnson
also said last Sunday, you have to say 'Thank you, Lord
Jesus, for dying for me'."

"I see," said Paul, again thoughtfully.

That night he lay awake thinking, long after Tony and

5

Richard were asleep. Finally he knew what he must do. He got up and knelt on his sleeping bag and prayed this prayer: "Thank you, Lord Jesus, for dying for me. I know that I am a sinner and I pray that You will take away my sin and make me a Christian."

As he climbed back into his sleeping bag, he thought to himself, "Well, now I am a Christian, I wonder what happens next. Will things be any different after this?"

He lay for a while turning the question over in his mind. He thought of those people who, as far as he knew, were not Christians, and then he thought of those whom he knew to be Christians, like the Challengers, the Johnsons, and all the workers at the mission. And, when he compared the two sets of people, it seemed to him that it was the Christians who seemed to be the happiest and most contented.

"Perhaps it will make quite a difference," he thought drowsily, and then dropped off to sleep.

CHAPTER XV

MORE ABOUT THE MISSION

THE week that followed was very full, and as it was the Challengers' and the Mission's last week the children made the most of it. Each day seemed to provide something special and Monday with a Workers' Hunt in the afternoon was no exception.

The idea was that all the workers should disguise themselves and mingle with the other people on the beaches and in the village; the children then had to look for them and, if they thought they saw them, challenge them with a password and obtain their signatures.

The children worked in couples but Elizabeth went round with her mother. Mrs. Challenger did not help her at all; if Elizabeth thought she saw a worker she would point her out to her mother, who would then approach and use the password which was, "Please excuse me, but my little girl wants to know if the water is over the causeway". Although she was only small, Elizabeth spotted about two-thirds of the workers and was thrilled to be given the tiny tots' second prize.

When the children got back to camp for tea and compared notes, they could not help laughing over some of the funny disguises the workers had used. Miss Wentworth had dressed up as a char and cleaned windows in the village, Mrs. Johnson had been a gypsy woman selling clothes pegs, while Miss Conway had simply tucked up her skirts, plaited her hair, and helped some unknown children to build a beautiful sand castle on the beach. Very few of the children had found Mr. Johnson who had put on workman's overalls, a dirty beret, and done some much-needed repairs to his car in a side street, and practically no-one had recognised Mr. Collier in his Scout uniform, cooking over a wood fire on the cliff. Most of the other disguises were more obvious and had been seen through by nearly all the children.

Tuesday was the Birthday of the Mission and a very special day. The sand pulpit for the day was nearly twice as large as it normally was, and was beautifully decorated. The Birthday text on it was 'Fear thou not, for I am with thee', and to go with it the children were taught a special Birthday chorus based on the same verse:

> 'Fear thou not, for I am with thee;
> Be not dismayed, for I am thy God;
> I will strengthen thee,
> Yea, I will help thee;
> I will uphold thee with my right hand.'

A special messenger from Mars, dressed in spaceman's clothes, delivered a parcel of birthday cards to be distributed to the children; these had printed on them the names and addresses of all the workers, and also the Birthday text and chorus, so that the children would not forget them. This messenger was also the special speaker for the day, and when he had removed his helmet and the other cumbersome articles of his spaceman's outfit, he spoke to them about the text and the chorus. He explained what they meant so clearly and simply that Paul, and other boys and girls who had become Christians during the Mission, knew that in this new life they had just started they would never be alone, but would have a constant Friend in the Lord Jesus Christ.

During the afternoon the Birthday Sports were held on the largest beach. There were races for all ages, including an obstacle race for the workers and a blindfold race for the parents. Elizabeth was the proud winner of the tiny tots' dressing-up race, arriving at the finishing tape in a very funny assortment of grown-up clothes, with Pauline a close second. All the other children won places in some of their races, but it fell to Colin Johnson to win the main intermediate prize as victor ludorum, much to the envy and admiration of Richard and Paul.

The prizegiving for the sports was held indoors in the evening and afterwards all the children were given a piece of birthday cake. They ate their own on the spot and as they went out were given a larger piece, wrapped up, to take home to their parents. As the Challenger party left, Mr. Johnson, who was directing the proceedings, said with a smile, "Only one for you Challengers, or you will all be having extra rations! Now who can we trust to take it safely?" and after a little teasing it was given to Elizabeth, as being the most trustworthy of them all!

Wednesday afternoon had been chosen for a treasure hunt, and though it was very hot this did not stop the children from racing round the village and sandhills nearly all the afternoon, chasing clues. None of the Challenger children were successful. It was usually the local children who won the treasure hunt as they seemed to know what places were meant almost before they had read the clues. Nevertheless, the children thoroughly enjoyed the afternoon and arrived back at the camp laughing and chattering about all they had done. Anne's partner had been a local girl but even that had not helped them to be earlier than fifth among the intermediates. The others were teasing her about this.

"Surely Gwen could do better than that, Anne. She's always lived in Banstone and knows all the places. I expect you held her back," said Richard.

"All right then, cocky!" retorted Anne. "But at least we

were fifth and not eleventh like you and Paul, and you are years older than us."

Mr. Challenger interrupted before they came to blows. "Well, out of the lot of you, didn't any of you distinguish yourselves? I don't think I shall bring you to Banstone again if that's how you disgrace me."

Anne flung herself on him. "Oh, Daddy! I think I should die if we didn't come back here again next year."

Tony giggled. "It would take more than that to finish Anne off."

Richard broke in. "Seriously, though, Daddy, are we coming here again next year? I don't think we've been to a nicer place, do you?"

"Your mother and I have just been talking about it this afternoon. Mr. Johnson was asking if we thought we should come back for a third year. What do the rest of you think about it? What about you, Paul?"

Paul flushed at being appealed to in that way as if he were one of the family. As once before when his opinion had been asked about their plans, he felt overwhelmed. It was awfully decent of Mr. Challenger to bring him in. Why, he might not even be coming with them again, though he very much hoped he would be invited and that his aunt would give permission.

"Well," he replied slowly, "I think Banstone is an absolutely wizard place, but I've not been to many places, you know."

At this point Mrs. Challenger called them all to tea and they continued to discuss the matter as they ate. They all seemed to think it a wonderful idea to come back again, but Mr. Challenger ended the discussion by warning them.

"Now, don't go counting on this. We can't possibly tell what we'll be doing in a year's time so you're not to be disappointed if it doesn't work out that way. Only we thought we would discuss it so that you can tell any of the workers and other children who ask you tomorrow when you say goodbye."

CHAPTER XVI

HANS AND GERDA

T HAT evening there were no special mission activities, and after tea, when Mrs. Challenger was getting Elizabeth ready for bed, the other children gathered round to discuss what to do before their bedtime. Suddenly they heard the latch of the gate click and saw, to their surprise, Hans and Gerda coming into the field. They hesitated when they saw the Challenger children and Paul, and looked at each other as if they did not know what to do. Their obvious embarrassment affected the others too, and the two groups of children stood staring awkwardly at each other for a moment. Then Richard broke the silence.

"Hullo, you two. Are you coming to see us?"

"Well, not exactly," said Hans. "We really wanted to see your father."

"Daddy? He's in the big tent. I'll fetch him," said Richard, but as he spoke, Mr. Challenger came out, saw the twins and came across the field.

"Hullo, twins. Are you coming to see us?" he asked, just as Richard had done.

The twins exchanged glances and then Hans, speaking with obvious effort, said, "We'd like to have a private talk with you please, sir."

"Why, of course." Mr. Challenger turned to the others and asked, "What were you going to do till bedtime?"

"We were just discussing it when the twins arrived," said Richard.

"Well, can we have the boys' tent to talk in? You can go

down to the beach till seven o'clock, if you keep your distance from the sea."

"Oh, thank you, Daddy," shouted Tony, as he rushed into his tent to get his bucket. "I want to try to get some fish in the rock pools. Are you others coming?"

They all collected buckets and were soon on their way down the path, leaving Mr. Challenger and the twins to have their talk.

"I wonder whatever the twins want," Paul said to Richard.

"Perhaps they've come to confess," speculated Richard.

"Confess what? Oh, you don't really believe they took those costumes, do you? Anyway, I've not noticed them at the meetings since the sausage sizzle on Friday, have you?"

"Yes, they were at the family service on Sunday, but they slipped away pretty quickly after. Perhaps their consciences pricked them when they saw it was Daddy giving the talk."

Paul said nothing. He remembered that it was that talk of Mr. Challenger's, and his private talk with him afterwards, that had made him decide to become a Christian. Things had been different since Sunday night. All the services were full of meaning for him now, and the Bible, which he had started reading himself each evening as Richard did, was beginning to come alive to him. He wondered if the twins wanted to talk with Mr. Challenger for the same reason as he had on Sunday.

They had a very happy hour, climbing the rocks and searching in all the pools, but they did not catch any fish, much to Tony's disappointment. The others had difficulty in tearing him away when it was time to get back to camp.

As they went through the gate into the field, Mrs. Challenger came out of the big tent to meet them.

"Have the twins gone?" asked Tony.

"Yes, Daddy has taken them back in the car, but he's bringing them back here to stay the night with us. They went in the car so as to be able to carry their stuff. Now, Anne and Tony, time to get ready for bed. Hurry, because you're later than usual. Anne, don't make a noise. Elizabeth is fast asleep. Tony, I've moved the beds up a bit to make room for Hans, and Gerda will come in with us."

"Oh, what fun, to have them staying with us," cried Tony, excitedly, and he and Anne went straight away to get ready without any of the usual protests that it was not bedtime, or that they were not a bit tired.

When they'd gone, Mrs. Challenger said to Richard and Paul, "You're old enough to know all about it and Daddy told me to tell you before they got back. Hans and Gerda came to see him, partly to tell him that they very much wanted to be Christians after his talk on Sunday, and to ask his help. He was able to help them and they both asked the Lord Jesus to come into their lives. But they also wanted to tell him that they are the ones that have been taking the food from the store tent and things off the line."

Paul and Richard exchanged glances. Mrs. Challenger noticed this immediately and said, "Why, what does that look mean?"

Richard explained. "Well, you see, Mummy, I thought I saw Hans drying himself with my towel after bathing one day last week. We didn't say anything because we thought it would be a bit mean unless we knew something a bit more definite. We tried to follow them another day after bathing but we lost them among the rocks quite a long way towards Penton."

"Yes, quite likely," said Mrs. Challenger. "Those two poor children have been camping by themselves in a cave for the past ten days. It seems they are Hungarian refugees and have been in a children's home in Mid-Wales for the past eighteen months. There was a new Matron a few months ago, who has treated the children very badly. Hans and Gerda seem to think she was particularly unkind to them but their unhappiness may be making them exaggerate. Whatever the case may be, if half what they say is true, then that woman ought never to have been sent to such a home. Anyway, they finally decided they could stand it no longer, and ran away ten days ago."

"But how did they get here, and how have they managed to feed and look after themselves all that time?"

"That's just the trouble. They emptied their money boxes and also stole some money from the home when they left. They walked quite a long way to a station not too near the home and then spent nearly all their money on the fare here. Then they had to take the things they needed as they went along. That's why they had our blankets and the various lots of food and clothes they've had from us and other campers."

Paul looked puzzled. "How did they come to pick on Banstone?"

"They saw a list of excursions in the station and there was a cheap day trip advertised to Banstone, and they had enough money for it, with a little to spare, so they chose that."

"But surely the police will be looking for them," said Paul again.

"Well, my husband will have to go into all that, of course, but meanwhile, he's bringing them over here for the night, with all the stuff they've accumulated, and we'll have to deal with all that side in the morning."

Not long after, Mr. Challenger and the twins returned with the car laden with odds and ends. Mrs. Challenger had cooked some bacon and eggs and made a big jug of cocoa.

"I don't suppose they've had a cooked meal since they left the home, poor things."

And it certainly seemed so. Hans and Gerda ate and drank ravenously all that was put before them, while Mr. and Mrs. Challenger made up beds for them and got out some spare night-clothes for them to wear. Mrs. Challenger had put on a large tub full of water to boil so that they could have a good hot wash, the first they had had for ten days. They had tried hard to keep themselves clean, but with only cold sea water and a small piece of stolen soap it had been almost impossible.

Later, when the three older boys had settled down in the ridge tent, with Tony fast asleep in the corner, Hans spoke shyly: "Your mother did tell you everything, didn't she, Richard?"

He nodded, and Hans went on.

"I'm most awfully sorry about the things we took of yours. You guessed about the towel after bathing that day, didn't you?"

"Richard noticed it," said Paul. "And we tried to follow you on Friday but we lost you among the rocks."

"Yes, I know," said Hans.

"You know! Did you see us then?"

"Yes, at least we didn't know it was you at first. We saw someone who seemed to be keeping up with us and, you know, not many people come along as far as that. That's why we picked a cave right along there. We went straight up the rocks to a little hiding-place we had discovered quite a bit higher up. We saw you come out and search for us so we waited there till you had gone off, and then came down and went to our own cave. We didn't want to give away our camping place."

"Oh, that explains it," said Richard. "We couldn't think what had happened to you."

"There's one thing I want to ask you. Why didn't you tell your parents when you suspected us?" asked Hans.

"Oh well," said Paul, slowly, "we weren't at all sure, you know, and we didn't want to make trouble till we knew definitely. And besides, you seemed such a sport, we didn't want to tell tales."

"Well, it's very sporting of you too," said Hans, smiling gratefully. He went on more slowly, "I think the worst of all this business has been the fear of being found out, and, of course, knowing that we were bound to be caught one day and perhaps made to go back to that horrible place."

"Oh, I'm sure Mr. Challenger will do all he can to help you, don't you think so, Richard?"

"Yes, I'm quite sure he will," affirmed Richard.

"Well, he's been most awfully decent already, in fact you all have."

To cover a slight awkwardness, Paul said, "I say, don't you think we'd better get to sleep now?" and all three of them wriggled down into their sleeping bags and were soon asleep.

CHAPTER XVII

LAST DAY

AFTER breakfast next morning, Mr. Challenger had a talk with Hans and Gerda.

"I think, after what you said last night, that you'd be glad to get this affair straightened out as soon as possible, wouldn't you? I'm afraid it means missing this morning's service and going round to the local police station."

"The police?" cried Hans, startled, and Gerda's eyes filled with alarm.

"Now, don't worry. You've nothing to be frightened of, if you tell the whole truth. But they'll have to have all those things you took to return to the various campers who have reported their losses. And they may have been told to look out for you. It must have been reported to the police by the home that you ran away, you know."

"Will we have to go back to that awful place?" asked Gerda.

"I can't say about that. But I will do my best for you both. And don't forget, there's a Father in Heaven who cares far more for you than I do. He won't let you down and whatever He decides will be best for you, even if it means going back to the home to face the music."

So it was a very subdued pair who left with Mr. Challenger for the police station at the same time as the others started to the beach for the service. As the Challenger children and Paul went down the path, the two older boys dropped behind to discuss Hans and Gerda.

"I wonder what the police will do" mused Richard. "It will be rotten for them if they have to go back to that awful home again."

"Yes, I know," said Paul, who knew, as Richard could never know, just how it felt not to have a real home. He had often wished he had parents at hand to turn to, and a home like the Challenger home where he felt he was really wanted. But what must Hans and Gerda feel who had no parents at all, and were so far away from their own country, and had no real prospect of returning?

Paul and Richard found it hard to concentrate on the service that morning. They were almost glad when it was announced that there would be no bathing afterwards, and they did their best to hurry the younger children back to the camp.

Hans and Gerda were sitting talking with Mr. and Mrs. Challenger, each drinking a glass of orange juice, and they looked considerably happier than they had done earlier.

When Richard opened the gate, Mr. Challenger came across to meet them all.

"Mummy's got some drinks," he said. "Anne, Tony and Elizabeth, you'd better go and get yours first, and tell Mummy that Richard and Paul will come in a minute."

When they had gone, he went on, "Everything's all right, in fact much better than we could have hoped. Apparently the Matron did not report that Hans and Gerda were missing for nearly a week, thinking they could not get far and would be hungry and come back. I don't know if she had a guilty conscience about the way she'd been treating them and thought it would all come out if she reported them missing. Anyway, her fears have been justified and there's to be an enquiry. Apparently one or two of the other staff have made public the way the home is run and how the children are treated, and the authorities are looking into it all. The Matron has been suspended until the enquiry is complete but it doesn't seem likely she'll be allowed back."

"How did you hear all this, Mr. Challenger?" asked Paul.

"Oh, I should have explained. The police have only just been notified that Hans and Gerda were missing, but when I explained matters, the Superintendent kindly rang up the police station nearest to the home to find out the whole situation."

"And what happens now, Daddy?" asked Richard.

"Well, they said the twins could stay here today but we have to put them on the train tomorrow morning."

"They won't be punished, will they?" asked Paul.

"No, they won't. And another thing, while I have you alone, I have an idea, but I don't want you to tell Hans and Gerda yet in case it comes to nothing. Richard, you know I am chairman of the committee of the children's home in Derwell? Well, I might be able to use my influence to have the twins transferred to that home and then we could see plenty of them, and make sure they're all right."

"Oh, that would be great!" exclaimed Richard. "It would be grand to have them so near. I think Hans is super, don't you, Paul?"

"Yes, he is," agreed Paul. "And I like Gerda too. She must be a sport to do all that camping out in a cave. Not many girls would stick that."

"Right," said Mr. Challenger. "Now go and get your drink, and mind, not a word to anyone yet."

The rest of the day was very happy, especially for Hans and Gerda, whose minds had been set so much at rest by what had happened at the police station.

The last afternoon was spent in a grand tidefight between the Banstone members of the mission and those from the rest of the country. For this special event everyone joined in, children, parents and workers, and many of the parents of local children turned up to help the Banstone team. The numbers in each team were about even.

Each team had to build the biggest and strongest sandcastle they could, quite near the water's edge. The tide was coming in and the castle which could best stand against it would be the winner. A Union Jack was to be planted in the top of each castle and the one that stood erect the longest would proclaim the winning team.

There was great excitement as everyone gathered in Smugglers' Cove at the beginning of the afternoon. It seemed as if the Banstone children had the advantage because many of the parents had brought along their garden spades, whereas most of the visitors, of course, had not brought theirs with them on holiday. The workers possessed two which were used each day for pulpit-digging, and one or two families, like the Challengers, who were having camping holidays had spades with them for all the necessary digging on the camp site. However, even with so many as they could muster, the visitors still only had about half as many spades as the Banstone people.

"Ah well," said Mr. Johnson, "we'll have to make up in hard work what we lack in the number of spades."

Colin, Richard and Paul, who had had their heads together in a serious discussion, came up to Mr. Johnson at this point.

"Daddy," said Colin, "what about building our castle around that bit of rock over there? It's well within the high water mark and you could use that to show where the castles are to be built."

"Well," said Mr. Johnson, "we've already decided that the castles should be built in line with where I am standing so as to give us about an hour for building before the tide comes in."

"Couldn't we do ours on the rock, even though it meant being nearer the sea and having less time to finish?" asked Richard.

"It would also mean that the sea would be washing round

6

our castle some time before the other one, you know. Do you think it's worth it?" asked Mr. Johnson.

The three boys conferred together for a moment and then Colin said, "I should think the advantage of being on the rock would make it well worth it, wouldn't you, Daddy?"

"I think you may well be right, Colin. But we'll have to ask the others if they have any objection. They might want to do the same."

Mr. Johnson walked over to Mr. Sandon, the leader of the Banstone team, who was the father of Gwen, Anne's partner in the Treasure Hunt.

"Our team is very anxious to build on that rock there," he said, "even though it is nearer the water line. How do you feel about that? Would you have any objection to that, or perhaps you'd like to use it yourselves?"

"No, that's all right as far as we're concerned. I was just going to say you ought to have first choice of site, as you are the visitors, and you have fewer big spades than we have."

"That's very hospitable of you," smiled Mr. Johnson. "Well, in that case, we'll take the rock itself to build round."

Then both teams set to work, marking out, digging, patting down, shaping, all working as hard as they could. The visitors' team could not hope to make their castle as big as the Banstone one, so they made sure to pat down each layer hard as it went on, and they did not waste any time in making their building beautiful. The Banstone castle certainly seemed to be very large, but the visitors were sure their own was as strong as they could possibly make it, and they hoped that, with that and the rock foundation, it would stand longer.

All too soon, the sea was beginning to lap against the base of their castle and they had to stop digging. Mrs. Johnson gave them a small Union Jack to put in the top of their castle and they all stood back to admire the result of their efforts. The Banstone team had an extra few minutes to put the final touches to their castle before the tide reached them and they planted their flag on the top.

The next half hour was most exciting. Everyone gathered round and, as the waves washed higher and higher up the castles, they could see pieces of each one washed away. The Banstone people felt sure of victory, but most of them forgot about the rock under the visitors' castle and they were dismayed when they saw that, although the waves were nowhere near the top of their castle, the base was crumbling badly with each wave that broke.

Suddenly a wave which seemed bigger than any they had seen all afternoon broke over both castles. Most of the base of the Banstone castle was swept away, the whole castle toppled over, and the flag was washed out to sea.

"Hurrah!" shouted the visitors. "We've beaten them."

"I think there's a parable in all this, don't you?" said Mr. Johnson. "What about ending with the chorus about it?"

So they all joined together and sang:

"Build on the Rock, the Rock that ever stands,
O build on the Rock, and not upon the sands;
You need not fear the storm or the earthquake shock,
You're safe for evermore if you build on the Rock."

There was a special farewell meeting at six o'clock which was called a Testimony Meeting, and one of the senior boys and one of the senior girls, as well as one of the workers, told how they themselves had become Christians. The senior girl lived in Banstone, had learnt about the Lord Jesus Christ through the Mission and had trusted Him at the Birthday Service three years before; the senior boy had become a Christian through the Christian Union in his boarding-school; and the worker, who was Mr. Stanton, had been brought up in a Christian family where the Lord Jesus was loved—like the Challenger family, as Paul immediately thought—and he had loved and trusted Him ever since he was quite a child. After the meeting ended everyone was asking and being asked whether they would be there next year and the Challengers felt that saying goodbye was not so bad because they could say they were hoping to be back again. But Hans and Gerda were different. It seemed as if they could not bear all the goodbyes, and they slipped quietly away, arriving back in camp before all the others.

On Friday morning, after breakfast and family prayers, the children all gathered round the car as Mr. Challenger drove off to the station with Hans and Gerda.

During that short journey, he talked to them quietly, reassuringly, reminding them of their new faith in Jesus Christ, and of God's love for each of them.

"I said yesterday He won't let you down. He has a particular plan for your lives and you can be sure it is the best that can happen to you, even though it may not seem so at the time. You have your Bibles at the home, and I want you to try to read them every day, using the cards and notes I gave you yesterday morning, and to pray each day, asking God's help and strength to live for Him."

Hans and Gerda nodded. They could not trust themselves to speak and Mr. Challenger understood and went on, as the car turned into the station drive.

"There's one other thing. Mrs. Challenger and I are going to try to arrange for you to come to stay with us as soon as possible. We are going to get in touch with the authorities about it straight away."

Hans' and Gerda's faces lit up at that, and when Mr. Challenger waved goodbye to them they were both looking quite cheerful.

When he returned, Mr. Challenger said to the children, "Well, they went off quite happily when I told them we're hoping they'll be able to come to stay with us at home."

"What are we doing today, Daddy?" asked Tony.

"I was just coming to that," said Mr. Challenger. "We want to get as much clearing up done as possible this morning so that we can get off in good time tomorrow. Then I vote that we go for a picnic to the causeway in the afternoon to finish off the holiday. Later on, the tide should be right for crossing it, for those who want to, and it will be fine for bathing earlier, too. All agreed?"

"Oo, yes!" cried the children in chorus.

"Well, mind you work properly this morning, because unless we've done all the jobs we can't go this afternoon. Understand?"

The children agreed and set to work with a will. Their clothes and personal belongings had to be sorted out and all packed in the big trunk except what would be needed on the morrow. The stores were dealt with in the same way, any unused tins being taken back to the grocer as he had agreed to refund the money on them. The store tent was then taken down and packed away and some of the other equipment with it. Most of that had to be kept, however, to use when striking camp in the morning. Everything possible was packed on the trailer of the car, and some of the things which had come by post were parcelled up again, and Richard and Paul took them to the post office. Everything was done to Mr. Challenger's satisfaction just as lunch was ready, and they all settled down to their last midday meal in camp with enormous appetites after their morning's work.

CHAPTER XVIII

FINAL PICNIC

SOON after lunch they all set out to walk to the cause-way, carrying with them their bathing things, a bat, a ball and a rubber ring, and, of course, their tea. It was not a very long walk and they arrived at three o'clock and de-cided to bathe straight away. The causeway was already uncovered and it would remain so for another three hours and the water would be too shallow for bathing in about half-an-hour. Everyone went in, but this time there were no practical jokes. Elizabeth was still rather nervous of the water and her parents had decreed that whenever she was bathing with them nothing should be done to frighten her. Nevertheless, it was a beautiful bathe, and seemed specially so to the children, because it would be their last sea-bathe for a whole year. The water at the causeway always seemed warmer than anywhere else and they stayed in until the tide had gone out so far that they could only paddle. Then, still in their costumes for it was very warm, they all played games on the sand—french cricket, rounders, their own form of 'halo' without a net, and other favourites. They had tea in their costumes and afterwards all changed back into their clothes, the children very reluctantly. They felt that this was really the last of their holiday. Just as Mr. Challenger was ready, Tony rushed up to him, hair standing on end, his collar half in and half out of his pullover, and the laces of his gymshoes knotted.

"I'm ready first! Daddy, can we go over the causeway before we go home? You said we could and it will be un-covered for ages yet."

"Just a minute, Tony. Did you say you were ready? What about your hair, shockhead, and those laces, too? It doesn't look as if you undid those when you undressed. And whatever have you done with your collar? I don't call you ready."

Tony looked injured. "Well, I haven't got a comb and I can't do my shoelaces and what's wrong with my collar anyway?"

"Only tucked down inside your pullover. Come on, son, let's straighten you up. There's my comb. You do your hair while I do these laces for you."

"Thank you, Daddy. But you will let us go over the causeway, won't you?"

"Well, I may take you. How would that do?"

"Oo, super! Will you really, Daddy?"

At this point Richard came up with Paul on the same errand.

"Richard, go and ask your mother what she and Elizabeth will do and ask Anne if she wants to come."

Richard sped off and came back in a minute saying, "Anne doesn't want to come and she and Mummy and Elizabeth will stay on for a bit and then walk slowly back to camp. We'll catch them up."

Mrs. Challenger and the girls followed Richard. Anne was rather afraid of the slipperiness of the causeway and of having a fall and this was why she had decided to stay with her mother. Mr. and Mrs. Challenger decided that they all ought to be back in camp by half-past six; there must be no one late in bed tonight, as they had to have an early start in the morning.

As Mr. Challenger and the boys went across the causeway, picking their way carefully to avoid slipping, Mr. Challenger said to Paul, "There's nothing to see on the other side but miles of sand, Paul. I can never understand why Tony and Richard are so keen on going across."

"Daddy!" cried Tony indignantly. "You know there are lots of pools left by the tide, and you never know what you might find in them. And I always like imagining that we're going to get cut off by the tide and be marooned, like on a desert island."

Mr. Challenger laughed. "It would only mean walking round by the bridge and it's a long walk too."

By this time they had reached the other side and began examining the pools left by the tide in hollows in the sand. As Mr. Challenger expected, there was nothing of interest in them but the boys spent a few moments looking in each one as if they expected to find hidden treasure. It was not until they had been walking across the sand for some time that Tony suddenly pointed a little way ahead and said, "Look Daddy! What are all those little things?"

Mr. Challenger's eyes followed where Tony was pointing and said, "I can't think, Tony," but then as he got nearer, "Why! they're jelly-fish, a whole lot of them. They've evidently been washed in by the tide."

"Are they alive, Mr. Challenger?" asked Paul.

"I shouldn't think so, or they wouldn't have been washed in like that. But make sure before you play around with them. They have a sting, you know."

The boys found pieces of brushwood and began turning the jellyfish over one by one to see if there was any sign of life. As Mr. Challenger had anticipated, they seemed to be dead but the boys insisted on looking at each one until Mr. Challenger looked at his watch and said, "Come on now. Time to be going back and we have to go quickly too. It's a quarter-to-six and the water will be up not long after six."

They went straight back across the sands towards the causeway, Tony leading the way. Suddenly he stopped dead and turned round, shouting, "Daddy, it's covered!"

"What! It can't be!" said Mr. Challenger and then he

looked at his watch and exclaimed, "My watch must have stopped. It still says a quarter-to-six and I don't know how long it's been like that!"

By this time they had reached the edge of the water and saw that it would be quite impossible to cross. The water was several inches above the causeway and there was quite a swift current which made it much too dangerous to attempt to cross.

Mr. Challenger turned to the boys and said, "I'm very sorry, boys. There's nothing for it but to walk by the bridge. And I'm afraid we must go at a steady pace. We must not be too late back. It should be an early night for all of us really." They set off walking alongside the water, going inland towards the bridge that crossed the river higher up. Gradually Tony and Richard dropped a little way behind and Paul found himself with Mr. Challenger, who grinned at him, saying, "A fine mess I've made of it, haven't I, Paul? I don't think Tony will be so keen on being marooned another time, do you?"

Paul laughed. "No, I don't think he will! Won't Mrs. Challenger be worried, though, Mr. Challenger?"

"No, I don't think so, Paul." He paused for a moment and then went on, "We make a point, she and I, of trying not to worry when things go wrong like this."

"Not to worry?" Paul was perplexed, thinking of how anxious and cross his aunt was if he got home late.

"Yes," replied Mr. Challenger quietly. "It's quite sensible really, if you think it out. Do you remember in family prayers today, and every day actually, how we committed the day to God and asked Him to watch over us? Well, He must know all about this and He must have a reason for allowing it to happen, too. And in addition, as soon as I realised about my watch, I prayed about it, asking God's help."

Again Paul was perplexed. "You prayed?"

Mr. Challenger smiled. "Oh, I didn't kneel down and pray, or even shut my eyes. But you know we can pray without doing that. At any time of the day or night we can pray, just where we are and whatever we're doing. Perhaps we need help and so we just say in our hearts 'Help me, Lord' or perhaps we want to thank Him for help He has given or for something specially nice that's happened to us and then we say, 'Thank you, Lord'."

This was quite a new thought to Paul and he was reassured by it. "I never knew that," he said to Mr. Challenger, and then went on, "Mr. Challenger, I shall miss family prayers terribly when I'm back home."

"Yes, I'm afraid you will, Paul," replied Mr. Challenger. "Especially if you're a Christian now. You are, aren't you?"

"Yes, I am," answered Paul, surprised. "How did you know?"

"Oh, you don't seem worried by things this week. You were worrying and thinking it all over last week, weren't you?"

"Yes. It was on Sunday night."

"Well, I'm extremely glad. Now about family prayers, I know you'll miss those but you can have your own Bible reading and prayer at home, you know. I'd like to give you a card, showing the daily portions we read, and some notes which will help you to understand the reading. And I expect you've learned quite a lot about how to pray this last fortnight, haven't you?"

"Yes," said Paul enthusiastically. "I'd no idea you could talk to God like that. I've only been used to church and school prayers before."

"Yes, you'll find it makes a difference. By the way, have you told Richard you're a Christian?"

"No. Should I?"

"Well, I'm sure he'll be thrilled to know, and it will make it more real to you. Look what a help it was to Hans and Gerda. It will also help you when you come to tell your aunt."

"My aunt? Have I got to tell her? She'll be ever so annoyed."

"I don't see why she should. If there's any real difficulty, you tell me about it and perhaps I could have a talk with her. But don't forget that the best way you can show you're really a Christian is in the way you behave. Do you remember the chorus we had at the farewell meeting last night?

Let it be seen that with Thee I have been,
Jesus, my Lord and my Saviour;
Let it be known I am truly Thine own,
By all my speech and behaviour."

"Yes, of course," said Paul thoughtfully.

By this time they had reached the road and, as they crossed the bridge, a car drew up beside them.

"Hullo, what are you all doing so far from home?" cried a voice they knew well. It was Mr. Johnson. "Can I give you a lift?"

"Why, we'd be very grateful," said Mr. Challenger. He beckoned to the two boys behind, who came running up and they all climbed in.

"Where have you been to, then?" Mr. Challenger asked Mr. Johnson.

"Oh, we didn't get all the parcels ready for the post in Banstone so I had to take them into Penton. The post office shuts later there, you know."

"Well, you're a real answer to prayer for us, anyway." Mr. Challenger turned and smiled at Paul, who understood and smiled back. He then went on to explain to Mr. Johnson what had happened to them and ended by saying," Do you mind stopping the car for a moment by the causeway. We left our stuff there to pick up on the way back."

"Oh!" exclaimed Richard, "I'd forgotten all about that!"

After that it did not take them long to get back to camp. Mr. Johnson dropped them at the end of the cliff path and they reached camp only ten minutes later than the time Mr. and Mrs. Challenger had agreed upon.

Elizabeth was already asleep in the big tent and Anne was nearly ready for bed.

"Time for you to get ready too, Tony," said Mrs. Challenger. "There's some milk for you and Anne when you're both ready. Richard and Paul, you have another half-hour before you get ready, so you can do what you like till then."

Richard and Paul decided to go and watch the moon coming up till it shone over the sea.

"It will be the last time we see such a sight for ages," said Richard, as they set off along the cliff path.

CHAPTER XIX

HOME

THE next morning the whole camp was up at six o'clock, and after a hot drink and a sandwich each they all set to work to strike camp. By breakfast time at eight-thirty, both tents were down and packed away on the trailer, the various pits had been filled in and the turf replaced, and there remained very little more to do.

Breakfast was a big meal and they were all extremely hungry after their early start. By ten o'clock they were ready to set off, but before they did so they all went down the cliff path to take a last look at the sea.

The journey home was a long one but was interspersed with plenty of breaks so that the children could get out and stretch their legs. They had elevenses, lunch and tea, and various odds and ends in between. In fact they seemed to do nothing but eat. At home they were not allowed to eat between meals but that rule was always relaxed on long journeys. They made good time and drove into Derwell shortly after six o'clock, depositing Paul at his aunt's house well before the promised time of six-thirty.

Paul had been more silent than the others on the journey, partly because the holiday had meant even more to him than it had to the Challenger family. It was the first family holiday he had ever had and the best he could ever remember, and he was very sorry it was over.

The previous night when he and Richard had gone down to watch the moon, he had begun to say shyly, "I say, Richard . . ."

Richard interrupted him. "I think I know what you're

going to say, Paul. Daddy has just told me you're a Christian too, now. Did you know I became one last year at the Mission?"

Paul was surprised. "No. I'd no idea you'd been one such a short time. I should have thought you'd have been one ages ago, in fact I don't see how you could help being one, with parents like yours."

"Well," replied Richard slowly, "I suppose I should have really, but I'm afraid I just didn't bother. When I did stop to think, I suppose I thought everything was all right because of Daddy and Mummy and going to church and everything. Perhaps it's possible to get too used to hearing about the Lord Jesus. In fact, I think it was someone saying just that at the mission last year that made me first sit up and take notice."

"Yes, but you know you are awfully fortunate to have a home like yours," said Paul. "I don't know how I'm going to get on by myself with reading the Bible and praying."

"Look, Paul," exclaimed Richard, "perhaps sometimes we could read our portions together and discuss any bits we don't understand, and I could tell you anything Daddy has said about them in the morning."

"I say, would you?" said Paul, gratefully. "I'm sure that would help."

"And," exclaimed Richard again, "perhaps there'll be a Christian Union at the grammar school. There are in some, you know, and we could join together and perhaps get some of the other boys and girls in our form to join too. And if Hans and Gerda do come to Derwell they might come to the grammar school, too, and they'd be sure to join."

Paul was thinking of all this during the journey home and he was thinking too of what he was going to say to his aunt and wondering what she was going to think. Then some of the things he had heard during the past fortnight flooded back to his mind. He was now a Christian and a follower of the Lord Jesus Christ, and though he knew that he would often fail Him, he knew too that the Lord Jesus would never let him down, or in the words of the Bible, would 'never leave him or forsake him'.

He stood at the gate and watched the Challengers' car out of sight; then he walked up the path slowly, saying in his heart, as Mr. Challenger had taught him to, "Help me, Lord". He let himself in quietly at the side door, knowing that his prayer would be answered.

Printed at the Press of the Publishers